Kate w...
ever m...

What was wrong with him? Other men dreamed of *Playboy* centerfolds, while Robert fantasized about a pregnant woman.

A gorgeous pregnant woman, the devil in him argued. *The woman pregnant with his child.*

At work every day he had to fight to keep his hands to himself. And now here in her home where she felt safe, all he could think about was carrying her off to the bedroom. Making love until both of them were spent.

He took a step toward her and Kate rose out of her chair. He stopped. He couldn't do this. He stepped closer and stopped. He *definitely* shouldn't do this.

"Oh, Robert," she murmured with a smile, closing the distance between them. He felt need and joy hit him simultaneously. Maybe Kate did care for him. With a groan he kissed her.

Woman. She tasted female and he couldn't stop himself from tasting her more deeply. Her sexy curves fit against his body perfectly. Soft female flesh against solid male torso. Kate moaned and he deepened the kiss.

He wanted to make love to her. Show her how good he could make her feel.

Tell her that she was *his* woman...

One of **Molly Liholm**'s favorite movies is *The Shop Around the Corner*, starring Jimmy Stewart and Margaret Sullavan. The story of two shop clerks who despise each other and then turn out to be each other's secret pen pal and potential lover is romantic, sentimental and yet utterly realistic and amusing. Using this comedy-of-manners premise, Molly has written a nineties version featuring a secret baby as the catalyst for bringing the two rivals together. Mayhem and diapers ensue!

A Toronto native, Molly worked in publishing for fourteen years before starting to write romance fiction. Look for many more funny, sexy stories from this talented new author!

Books by Molly Liholm

HARLEQUIN TEMPTATION
552—TEMPTING JAKE

BOARDROOM BABY
Molly Liholm

Harlequin Books

TORONTO • NEW YORK • LONDON
AMSTERDAM • PARIS • SYDNEY • HAMBURG
STOCKHOLM • ATHENS • TOKYO • MILAN
MADRID • WARSAW • BUDAPEST • AUCKLAND

For my mother, Elsie Vallik, who shared with
me her love of books,
And my father, Heino Vallik, who gave me his
love for telling a good story.

ISBN 0-373-25743-0

BOARDROOM BABY

Copyright © 1997 by Malle Vallik.

1

"THE RABBIT DIED."

Hearing the words that for so long had been her secret code, Kate Ross sank into the soft butter-yellow leather of her executive chair. "Oh." The exclamation came out as a sigh. She'd been hoping for exactly that information from her friend, Dr. Ellen Chase, but the reality was still a shock.

"Kate, are you still there?" Ellen demanded over the phone.

Kate straightened her back and grasped the receiver more tightly in her sweaty palm. "Yes, I'm fine. Just a little overwhelmed."

"I should have had you into the clinic to tell you face-to-face," Ellen said, "but I know how busy your schedule is and how anxious you were to find out right away, so I broke a few rules. Still, you're going to have to slow down that busy vice-president pace."

"I'm not a vice president yet," Kate told Ellen unnecessarily. Ellen knew all about her corporate struggles, and the vice presidency that was almost within her grasp.

She swiveled her chair around, away from the corner-office view of the industrial complex below, to survey what she did have—the corner office. The yellow striped wallpaper with blue flowers complemented the light blue couch and the yellow-hued chairs. The vivid slashes of emerald and violet in the pillows on the sofa, as well as the tapestry wall hanging added color, while the polished mahogany desk and tables just oozed with success. Her desk was solid but not domineering. Kate had worked hard to create a business environment in which people would still realize she had no pretensions of becoming one of the guys.

In the old-boys' firm of Carlyle Industries—named after the founders' two sons, Carl and Lyle, and none of his four daughters—it wasn't easy, but her hard work and smarts had paid off. Director of marketing, Western Division, and she had only one real competitor for the vice presidency. Soon she could be vice president, Marketing, of Carlyle Industries, the third-biggest manufacturer of consumer household goods in North America.

"Kate, are you still there?" Ellen's words interrupted Kate's daydreams. She held a palm against her stomach and quelled her sudden wild urge to dance around the office. Her dream—her other dream—was about to come true.

"Ellen, you're the best doctor in the whole world," Kate said, meaning every word. She pulled out her calendar to schedule her next appointment. "When do you want me in?"

Ellen suggested a date two months away, when Kate had been scheduled to attend focus groups in Dallas. "No problem," Kate assured her. Her new life was going to require some rearranging of her priorities, but it wasn't anything she couldn't handle. At the moment, she felt like Superwoman. Thanking Ellen again, she hung up.

Throwing out her arms, Kate kicked the floor with one leg to spin her chair round and yelled, "Whee!" Not exactly the appropriate behavior for an executive, Kate knew, but at the moment she didn't care. For one instant she would just be herself.

"Did the Big A make the announcement?" Jennifer Givens asked from the doorway. Her tone conveyed amusement and sophistication—and so did Jennifer herself. If Grace Kelly had decided to crash through the corporate glass ceiling, only she might have done it as coolly and effortlessly as Jennifer. From the first day Kate had joined Carlyle Industries, she'd liked and admired Jennifer. They'd quickly grown close.

Kate slapped both feet on the ground to stop her spinning chair and watched her best friend as she closed the door behind her. For Kate, who at the best of times had to admit her personal style was eclectic, Jennifer was the personification of elegance. Today she was wearing a navy pant suit with gold trim and white spectator pumps. Somehow Jennifer always managed to combine conservatism with panache. Certainly no executive vice president had ever raised an eyebrow over Jennifer's clothing. Which, Kate admitted with chagrin, was more than could be said about herself. Oh, she'd tried the blue power suits with the prim, white blouse and the piece of polka-dot silk as a tie wanna-be. But with her first significant promotion, she had thrown out each piece of corporate conformism.

Too bad Jennifer had never been able to pass along her polish to Kate, she reflected with regret. Today Kate had on a favorite yellow silk blouse with orange linen slacks. Her shoes were burnt orange nubuck. While she owned a jacket that matched the pants, she had decided to think neutral and wear a cream-colored jacket. Giving Jennifer the once-over, Kate realized that she hadn't accomplished the look she'd intended.

Kate loved to shop. Every time she entered a store, she swore to stick to the neutrals, but when she came back out her bags were filled with a peacock tail of colors. She never worried about a particular shade of canary or magenta matching something in her closet because, well, there was so much in her closet that *something* was bound to work. If not, she could always buy a new piece that would be perfect.

In fact, at the end of Kate's first week, Jennifer had welcomed her to Carlyle Industries by inviting her out for dinner and shopping along Chicago's Magnificent Mile. Jennifer had joked that the male executives could bond at their men-only golf club in Oak Park, but that she and Kate would have more fun bonding in the fine female traditional way. When Jennifer had scooped the last fuchsia Donna Karan jacket off the sale rack for Kate, an eternal friendship had been formed.

Kate wasn't sure what she would have done without Jennifer, who was so much more balanced than she was. When Kate was running off in too many directions simultaneously, Jennifer always pulled her back to what was most important.

This was sort of what Jennifer did at Carlyle. She

was a great company spokesperson, but she also made sure the firm had a social conscience—contributing corporate funds and staff time to various charities. She and Jennifer had taken great satisfaction in convincing Anderson to quit the company's sponsorship of the male-only country club.

It was Jennifer's personal life that Kate worried about. Jennifer might look cool and sophisticated, but she had a big heart—one that had been broken too many times. After her last disastrous love affair, with a married man it turned out, Jennifer had built a shell around herself, retreating into her career. She didn't seem to have any dreams left for herself.

Jennifer regarded her expectantly. "Are congratulations in order?" she inquired.

"Yes, but not because Anderson promoted me—or Devlin," she hastened to add. She searched for words and then decided to use the code they'd been using ever since she had first confided in Jennifer. "The rabbit died," Kate said flatly.

Jennifer turned pale. "You're pregnant. You're really pregnant," she said in a shocked whisper. She shook her head, her shiny blond bob swinging back and forth. "I can hardly believe you really did it. I mean, I knew you were planning to, that you wanted—that you went, but—"

Kate poured a glass of water from the carafe on her desk and quickly handed it to Jennifer who gulped it down. Kate had never seen her friend so flustered.

"I'm sorry Kate. I'm not being a very good friend."

Jennifer put down the empty glass, stood up and held her arms wide open. "Congratulations."

Gratefully, Kate went into her best friend's embrace, suppressing her momentary worry. If Jennifer—who had been with Kate every step of the way—was taken aback with the news of her pregnancy, how was everyone else, her family, her co-workers, Larry Anderson, going to receive it?

Nothing to worry about, she told herself. A single mother was no longer cast out of society, with a red *M* for mother emblazoned across her chest. Especially a successful, rational, mature woman like herself. At thirty-six, it was past time to be a mother. And while being a *single* mother had never been her first choice, it hadn't been a frivolous decision. She'd hoped to be married. She'd even been engaged to be married. But since she was single, she'd made a responsible decision. She liked the sound of that—*responsible decision*. She'd have to use that phrase when she told Larry Anderson.

The thought made her feel faint and she sat down in one of the wing chairs.

It wasn't as if she couldn't afford to have a child— heck, she could afford two if she happened to be carrying twins or she decided to have another one. Coming from a large family, Kate believed being an only child was too lonely. Especially if there was just one parent. If everything went well, she planned on having a second child. But seeing the incredulous look on Jennifer's face as she stared at Kate's flat stomach, Kate decided not to remind Jennifer of the possibility just now.

A baby! A soft, baby-smelling baby.

With little baby hands and little baby feet.

Who would go to sleep in her arms and wake up looking for her mommy.

Kate could hardly believe it was real.

A baby was as important to her as her corporate success. And now she finally had it—she was pregnant. In just seven and a half months, in less time than it would take to get her baby-food campaign off the ground, she, Kate Ross, was going to be a mother.

She really was going to have it all.

Kate knew she could afford the best medical care and hire an excellent nanny. Her parents didn't live all that far away, but she didn't want to dump a child on them either. Recently they had been talking about selling their house in Chatham and moving into the city. Her parents, retired and child free, wanted to experience living in downtown Chicago and Kate hoped they would. They deserved their own life.

No, she could handle it all by herself. And she was on the verge of achieving her other dream—vice presidency. All that stood in her way was Robert Devlin, director of marketing, Eastern Division. He was the toughest competition she'd ever faced, but she was confident in her skills and her team. Devlin's challenge was only making her stronger.

No, Kate Ross wanted it all.

And she was sure she could get it.

"Oh, Kate," Jennifer said with a sniff, "I'm so happy for you." She burst into tears.

Kate hadn't seen Jennifer cry since her friend had received her own vice presidency two years before. As the only female with that title at Carlyle Industries, Jennifer had maintained a stoic facade throughout the momentous day, even as other women at the company, overwhelmed by the sign of progress, had wept openly. It wasn't until after the celebratory dinner, when Kate had returned to Jennifer's house for one last drink, that Jennifer had burst into tears. Knowing how softhearted Jennifer was under her professionalism, Kate hadn't been surprised, instead she'd joined her.

The fact that Jennifer was crying now, within the corridors of Carlyle Industries, shocked Kate. Feeling overcome, her spine weakened and she felt herself slump farther down in her seat. Her friend's emotional outburst suddenly brought the stark reality of Kate's situation home to her. Kate gazed ahead unseeingly. What had she done?

Becoming a single mother through artificial insemination was the stupidest, craziest thing she'd ever done.

Whatever had possessed her?

She imagined the horrified face of Larry Anderson. Robert Devlin's satisfaction. Her mother's shock. For a minute she let the images wash over her.

But then she pictured the baby again.

Would the baby be bald or have hair? Her sister Anne's little boy had been born with a halo of dark hair that he'd lost after a few months. After that, with his funny expressions and hairless head, he'd looked like a wise old man but Kate had never shared her impression with her sister.

And now she was going to have her own child. She stifled her anxieties and sent up a silent prayer of thanks.

Maternal instinct—strong and simple—was what drove her. When she and Todd had split up six months ago, Kate realized that waiting for the right man to come along could take forever. Oh, she still hoped that a suitable, comfortable man was out there somewhere, and that she'd find him. But she wasn't the kind to wait passively. She'd been engaged twice, once to her college boyfriend who, it turned out, didn't really want her to be a successful career woman. That relationship had quickly ended. Todd Miller had been a different story. They'd been together for almost three years. Everyone had been waiting for them to announce their engagement. It was only after they had set the wedding date that she and Todd had realized they were better friends than lovers.

Actually, Todd had realized it first. Kate had realized it after he'd ended their engagement.

She could recall his words perfectly. How he respected her, liked her, even loved her. How well their personalities, ambitions and goals meshed. But that he'd realized he wasn't totally, completely and overwhelmingly in love with her. That if they didn't spend the rest of their lives together, he wouldn't be overcome with misery. And to his own surprise, that was what he wanted.

She'd been speechless. Not because Todd's leaving her would devastate her—he was right about their comfortable relationship—but that Todd was such a romantic.

That he was capable of such passion.

She had to admit, they had never experienced it together. Their sex life had been good but never anything more.

Todd still called her occasionally, although it had been several weeks since she'd heard from him. They had a lot of friends in common so they occasionally ran into each other. They had danced together at the Westport Health Club's Christmas party and Todd had congratulated her on convincing Carlyle Industries to choose the Westport for their new corporate membership.

No, it was a very civilized breakup. Because she hadn't wanted an engagement ring—she'd preferred an impressive wedding ring with sapphires and diamonds—many people at work didn't even know that she and Todd were no longer a couple.

Todd had been right about them. His actions six months ago had also forced her to admit that the only aspect of their relationship she had been passionate about was her desire to be a mother.

Once she'd admitted that, she knew what she had to do. She would *become* a mother. Luckily, her good friend, Ellen Chase, was a doctor at a fertility clinic. After weighing all the pros and cons, Kate had had herself artificially inseminated.

And now...she was pregnant!

She had a sudden urge to go home and begin work

on the nursery immediately. Pink or blue? Or a neutral color? Should she ask about the sex of her baby?

A knock sounded at her door. Without waiting for a response, the last person she wanted to see entered. "I have the budget forecasts, and your numbers on promotion seem excessive, so I thought—" Robert Devlin raised his head from the printouts and looked from Jennifer's tear-stained face to Kate's bemused expression. He dropped the printout on the glass coffee table, sat next to Jennifer and took one of her hands in his. "Can I help?" he asked.

Jennifer's eyes met Kate's for a confused second but then she looked down to her and Robert's clasped hands and gracefully removed her hand from his. Kate watched as Jennifer smoothed an imaginary wrinkle from her trousers and transformed back into a corporate professional. When she raised her eyes to Devlin's concerned ones, her calm mask was in place. "Thank you," Jennifer said as she squeezed his hand and then released it. "Kate was sharing some good news with me. I believe I must be overtired to have reacted so emotionally."

Devlin's gaze darted to Kate.

"Don't look so worried, Devlin," Kate said dryly as she leaned over to pick up the printout. Numbers, spreadsheets and marketing reports were his life. She was surprised that he was capable of showing concern for Jennifer. But then, Jennifer was irresistibly beautiful. Even iceman Devlin had to have some kind of reaction to her. "The news was purely personal. Don't worry, the vice presidency is still open."

"Kate, that's unfair. Robert was being kind," Jennifer rebuked her gently. She and Kate had never agreed on Devlin. Jennifer had some crazy notion that Devlin was actually a kindhearted, giving person. She claimed Kate misunderstood him.

Kate understood him only too well. He was driven and ambitious the way she was. As far as she could tell, he had no personal life. When she worked late, which occurred frequently, he was also there. More annoying, he was still hard at it when she left.

His analyses of projects was brilliant, but he was cold. He never smiled. When she won over boardrooms with her wit and charm, he sat unmoving— waiting with his tough questions to close in for the kill.

She didn't mind that, but his lack of enthusiasm, his lack of passion irked her. She went out of her way to get a rise out of him but it never worked. He was her fiercest competitor but their styles were completely different. She led her team with her vision, creativity and enthusiasm. He prodded, analyzed and nitpicked. She leaped intuitively, trusting her instincts. He calculated and proceeded cautiously. He drove her crazy, but she didn't seem to affect him at all. Not something she was used to.

Kate calculated she and Devlin were running neck and neck for the promotion. Benson and Silver were the dark horses. Diamente also had a chance.

At the idea of being vice president, Marketing, North America, a little thrill went through her. Carlyle Industries manufactured more convenience-food products, household cleaners and supplies than most consumers were aware of. The company wanted the average person using Carlyle products exclusively—from cereal and toothpaste in the morning, to microwavable dinners and instant caffe latte in the evening. And soon they'd also have the baby-food market cornered. Carlyle's ambition was to go from third, to first place, and Kate hoped to help make that a reality.

Jennifer stood. Devlin did, too. He was annoyingly polite like that. Do-the-right-thing Devlin, Kate called him. "I have a press release to finish. I'll leave you two to fight," Jennifer said as she made her way out of Kate's office.

"We don't fight," Kate insisted.

"Disagree loudly then," Jennifer retorted and smiled. For some reason, Jennifer was amused by Kate and Devlin. Kate couldn't see why. Jennifer definitely had a soft spot for him. She was the only person who called him Robert.

"Nonsense, Jennifer. Ms. Ross and I may disagree on our approach to problems, but we're both interested in compromise," Devlin said.

"Speak for yourself," Kate disagreed, staring at the printout. "There is no compromise on the promotion numbers." She couldn't believe he wanted to cut the budget.

"Ridiculous, you've exceeded even your own previous inflated estimates." Devlin pulled out his glasses, put them on and flipped to the third page. Kate had often noticed that Devlin used his glasses like a weapon. When he put them on, he meant serious business; gesturing with them meant he was furious. If Devlin had been a vain man, Kate would have been convinced he used them for effect, but while he dressed in expensive, well-tailored suits, crisp white shirts and understated ties, Kate knew he could care less about how he looked. He simply bought the best. When Jennifer had commented that his rugged dark looks were extremely appealing, Kate had been surprised. She wouldn't call Devlin ugly, but certainly he had none of the style, the flair of the men she was attracted to.

She'd asked Jennifer if she planned to seduce Devlin, but Jennifer had only laughed and declared she wasn't his type. The truth was, no one was Jennifer's type these days. Clearly, Devlin's reaction to Jennifer's distress showed that he was interested. Still, Kate could not imagine the two of them together.

"Here. Silver's numbers are much lower." Devlin interrupted her musings.

"That's because Silver thinks conservative estimates make him look good. We've got to spend bucks if we want to make bucks," Kate insisted.

"Not if it bankrupts us in the process. I've run a new forecast. We can still reach eighty-five percent saturation by reducing your numbers by forty percent."

"Forty percent! That can't be done," Kate asserted.

"Have fun, you two," Jennifer said in her amused voice from the doorway.

Kate barely looked up to wave goodbye to her friend. The only fun she'd have would be to rip up Devlin's printout and sprinkle it over his bowed head.

2

DEVLIN TOOK OFF his glasses, folded the arms closed and placed them in front of him on the boardroom table. He pushed them slightly to the left where they would be perfectly aligned with his portfolio.

He smoothed his finger along the highly polished wood of the oak table. He liked Carlyle's corporate boardroom. The smaller meeting rooms on the other floors reflected the departments that used them—the casual disarray the art department favored, the sleek glass and chrome of Finance—but the corporate boardroom represented everything he admired about Carlyle Industries. The wing chairs in restrained, respectful colors. The solid, well-crafted table. Even the bust of the company's founder gave the place a sense of history, of continuity. Of family.

He knew that no one else suspected that for him Carlyle was home and family. Here, he'd been accepted. Here, he fit in. He knew a great deal about all of the Carlyle employees and whenever he could, he helped them. They were his responsibility.

Except for Kate Ross. She had arrived on the scene like a trendy new soda flavor, and, unfortunately, she had caught on. She just didn't understand the importance of standards and rules—of learning everything she could before making changes. Devlin knew the company needed to react faster, to become a little more visionary, but these things took time. You couldn't upset all the old boys at once. You had to give a little, too.

Devlin glanced at his watch in irritation. The weekly 9:00 a.m. wrap-up meeting was standard procedure for all senior executives. Its brief agenda was an opportunity for the decision makers to discuss ideas or thrash out issues before they became problems. When he'd joined Carlyle Industries five years ago, these meetings had been one of the first changes he'd initiated.

All sitting in their usual chairs were Silver, Benson, Swinson, Givens—Jennifer smiled at him when she noticed him looking at her—Lockwood, Lipp and Diamente. Everyone except Ross. Devlin frowned. She was more than ten minutes late and he refused to be delayed by her bad manners any longer.

To his left, Harold Silver, tall and thin with a mop of gray hair, leaned over and whispered, "She was late for Wednesday's focus-group debriefings, as well."

To his right, Eric Benson smiled sourly. "Looks like our rising star is losing her shine. Her reports have been consistently behind schedule for the last four weeks." He kept his voice quiet so that Jennifer couldn't hear him, and Devlin wondered why he had never noticed how much the man resembled a rat, with his high shining forehead and twitching nose. "Even more, the competition has been affecting her nerves." Benson moved in closer and Devlin backed off as far as the chair would let him, "Gina, my secretary, found

Kate in the bathroom throwing up yesterday morning."

Silver and Benson smiled unpleasantly as Devlin's respect for them dropped a few notches. Normally, Silver and Benson didn't bother him too much, but the competition for the vice presidency was pulling out the worst in them.

But, Kate, with her breezy attitude, her belief that she could charm her way through any situation—which she almost always could—was the only individual who really irked him.

Just then Kate rushed in, but the last thing he'd call her entrance was breezy. Pale, with large circles under her eyes, she apologized for her tardiness then sat down in her chair. And didn't say more than a few words throughout the entire meeting.

Of course, she still managed to charm everyone. Nor could any man fail to appreciate her long legs or pretty face. Kate didn't use her feminine appeal, but a man would have to be dead not to notice.

Devlin, chairing the meeting, asked her opinion once or twice. She answered competently, but he was convinced that only a small part of her was paying attention. It was only when Benson tried to work his way onto the From Mother's Kitchen project that she raised her head, smiled sweetly and assured him her workload was fine. When she said only that and didn't put Benson in his place, Devlin knew something was definitely wrong.

Kate was the first out of the meeting, which was like her, she always had a hundred projects on the go, so

Devlin walked with Benson to his office. There he asked him for the 1996 figures for the Eastern Seaboard.

Benson waved a hand. "Ask Gina for them, I have no idea where she keeps them."

"Thanks." With his hand on the door, Devlin turned back to Benson. "I read over your marketing plans for Carlyle soaps and thought most of your ideas were excellent, although the ad agency seems to be proposing a very conservative approach."

Benson turned a little pink as his nose twitched—it always did when he was about to lie. "Tell me about it. I've tried again and again to tell them that we want something more contemporary, but..." He threw his hands up dramatically.

Knowing full well it was Benson's apprehensions that inhibited the ad agency, Devlin smiled and decided how to best deal with the problem. "Maybe I could have Gina schedule a meeting between you, me and the agency and we could present a united front to them?" he suggested mildly.

"Oh, yes, er...excellent. Just have Gina remind me. Sometimes the girl forgets to enter appointments on my calendar."

Devlin closed the door behind him, grimacing. He knew that Benson's missed meetings were due to the company golf-club membership at the new club—he had to give Jennifer and Kate credit for dragging Carlyle into the twentieth century—not Gina's carelessness. Benson snuck out of the office to play whenever he could, which was frequently.

At the sound of a pencil snapping in two, Devlin turned toward Gina.

"Girl!" she snarled, and glared at Devlin. He winced and saw that the pencil Gina had bisected was a plastic, refillable one. Marveling at her strength—and her ability to work for Benson—he approached her desk.

"How are Rose and Jason?" he asked, to take her mind off Benson. Gina, a petite brunette, doted on her children. A collage of pictures of the six-year-old Jason, dark-haired like his mother, and his eight-year-old sister covered her bulletin board. He noticed a new one of the blond girl grinning to reveal two missing front teeth.

Gina, noticing his attention, smiled and said with a sigh, "She gets to be more like her father every day— all charm and trouble. She lost those two teeth in a fight with a ten-year-old boy."

"How badly was the boy hurt?"

"Two black eyes," Gina admitted ruefully. "Rosie is a fighter."

"Just like her mother. Alan Blackwood told me the detectives tracked down your ex and the courts garnisheed his wages for child support."

"Oh, yes." When Gina turned grateful eyes on him, he shifted uncomfortably. "Mr. Blackwood has even managed to collect some of the back child-support payments and thinks we'll be able to get the rest soon. Which is a good thing, because at this rate Rosie is going to need braces."

Gina frowned and bit her lip, an uncharacteristic sign of uncertainty. "What is it, Gina?"

"It's Mr. Blackwood's bill."

"The bill?" Devlin asked innocently, dreading what was coming next.

"There isn't one! Mr. Blackwood put in a lot of work and time and did way better than those legal-aid lawyers, but he says I don't owe him any money. It's just not right," she said indignantly.

"Er...no, yes. Alan Blackwood is a friend of mine—"

"And I really appreciate you asking him to help me, but I'm not a charity case, Mr. Devlin."

"Of course not, Gina, but as I said, Alan is a very good friend and he makes an excellent living off his corporate clients. Some cases he likes to win just because it's the right thing to do." Devlin stopped, hoping he'd convinced Gina. She looked skeptical but didn't say anything else. Devlin was thankful because he knew he wasn't a very good liar. In business negotiations he could put on a poker face and switch numbers faster than a trickster can switch a peanut under the shell, but in a personal situation...

He understood Gina's pride but couldn't let that stop him from trying to help her. Alan might be his oldest and only friend, but Alan couldn't do all his work for free—not with his growing family to support. Devlin had given Alan a substantial retainer—not nearly enough to cover what Alan could have charged—and then Alan had refused to accept any more. Devlin had called him a damn fool and given him a check to cover the remaining expenses, but Alan had ripped it up, announcing that Devlin wasn't the only one with a conscience. But conscience had nothing to do with it; it was simple economics. Devlin made a very good salary, had few extravagances, so why shouldn't he spend his money where it would do some good?

"Benson said you'd have the 1996 figures for the East Coast."

"Sure. It'll take me a minute." Gina rose from her desk and walked over to the file cabinets.

Devlin leaned against her desk, watching as Gina bent down and opened one of the lower drawers. She really was quite an attractive woman—in a bright-eyed, open-faced way. He wondered, not for the first time, why any man would abandon a wonderful woman like Gina and their children. And then refuse to take responsibility for them. He knew it happened all the time, but he would never understand it.

"Do you really need this report or is this just a trick?" Gina asked, looking over her shoulder at him.

He started guiltily. Gina couldn't possibly know he wanted to question her about Kate Ross. "A trick—"

"To watch my rear as I bend over like this," she teased.

Devlin felt heat rise up his face as Gina continued. "Oh, don't be silly Devlin. Everyone knows you're not that sort. Here," she stood and handed him a thick file. "If there's anything specific you want, I could do an analysis," she offered. Getting onto the management track was Gina's wish, Devlin knew.

"Not this time," he said. When her smile dropped, he added, "But we're putting together a team for the revitalization of our soap campaign. I could put your name forward."

"Would you? That would be just the opportunity I've been looking for. Thank you."

At her radiant smile, Devlin felt a little guilty about his plan to question her about Kate, but he had to know the truth. "I understand you helped out Ms. Ross when she wasn't feeling well the other day."

"Oh, it was nothing," Gina said, waving the experience off.

"I hope it wasn't the cafeteria food from lunch," he probed.

"It couldn't have been, she was sick early in the morning. I think Ms. Ross had just been working too hard, and what with her being here at seven-thirty—" everyone at Carlyle Industries knew that Kate Ross did not like the early morning "—she'd probably just done too much," Gina said.

"I'm sure you're right. Thanks for the report." Devlin turned, ready to leave.

"Mr. Devlin..."

"Yes?" he said as he turned back to her.

Gina looked nervous for a minute then said in a rush. "I just wanted to say thank you. For *everything*," she added meaningfully, and Devlin knew he hadn't fooled her about the lawyer's fee. "Without your help, I don't know what I would have done. There's one more thing, Mr. Devlin." Gina looked down at her desk and took a deep breath before meeting his gaze. "Could I call you Robert? Not here in the office, of course, but if we should meet outside..."

Devlin knew he was blushing but couldn't do anything. "Sure. I'd like it if you called me Robert. Here, too."

"Oh, not here. It wouldn't be appropriate. But outside, I'd like it if you considered me your friend." Gina sat down at her desk and turned her attention to her computer screen as if she knew how awkward real emotion was for Devlin.

HOURS LATER, Devlin took off his glasses and rubbed his eyes.

"You work too much," Mrs. deVito announced as she emptied his wastepaper basket into a large disposal bin. She pushed it aside and began to clean the coffee table.

"We all work too hard. It's the nineties," he answered. He'd been waiting for the cleaner's arrival. She'd been with the firm that cleaned Carlyle offices for a long time and she was extremely observant. He was hoping she, too, would have noticed the changes in Kate Ross. "It's a good thing for me I love my work."

"You should be home with a nice girl and family," she chided, beginning her favorite discussion.

"Not tonight, Mrs. deVito." Devlin held up a hand in defense.

"Hmmph," the older woman snorted. "You won't find a nice girl to marry if you're always behind that desk." Her well-worn face softened as she continued, "My Antonio and I have had over forty happy years together so far."

"Not everyone is meant to be married," Robert said mildly.

She frowned. "You say that because you don't know what you're missing."

"Perhaps that's true, but I am quite content with my life." He fiddled with his glasses, wondering how to broach the topic. He knew a lot about the older woman's family, and she knew about him via her own questioning, but he had never asked her for a favor before. "Mrs. deVito, I wouldn't ask if it wasn't important, and I can't tell you why right now, but I'm concerned about Ms. Ross."

"Go ahead and ask. I know you're a good man." Her face softened and her eyes grew misty. "A million thank-yous for helping Victorio get into the intern program. He's so happy."

"You're welcome." Robert cut her off before she could expand further. Mrs. deVito was quite capable of going on for a good ten minutes over the virtues of her oldest son and how important the job was. Robert should know, he'd heard it often enough and been the recipient of many frozen home-cooked meals. The dinners were wonderful, but he found Mrs. deVito's gratitude overwhelming. All he'd done was write a letter of recommendation.

"The spinach ravioli you left for me last night was excellent—Tony's downtown doesn't make it any better." Mrs. deVito blushed at the comparison to the famous restaurant on Michigan Avenue, and Devlin pressed his advantage. "About Ms. Ross..."

She nodded her gray head vigorously and said,

"Yes. Yes. There's another one who works too hard. At least she has that nice fiancé." She stared at him pointedly. "You make sure her young man knows. *Soda crackers.*" She grabbed his coffee cup. "You drink too much of this. I'll wash it out. I've left a nice cannelloni in the fridge for you. I also have a very pretty niece who's coming to visit Chicago. I could introduce you."

"Mrs. deVito, you don't need to cook for me. I'm a grown man perfectly capable of looking after myself." He ignored her suggestion of a blind date. Over the years, he'd learned that was the best tactic to use with the determined matchmaker.

"Hardly," she announced, and laughed.

Devlin shook his head ruefully as she wheeled her cart out of his office. He could hear her laughing all the way down the hall.

He frowned. He didn't like what he was thinking—how tired and different Kate had been recently. Throwing up in the morning. The soda crackers... All the clues pointed to one thing, but he needed to find out for sure. He stood and put on his suit jacket. The report he was working on could wait until tomorrow. He put the advertising campaign for Benson's soap revitalization campaign in his briefcase and picked up Mrs. deVito's pasta from the executive kitchen.

He stopped in the hallway, next to the elevators. He could just push the button and leave. Not involve himself.

Instead, he found himself walking down the hall to Kate's office. Her door was open and light spilled out. He stopped and looked in. Kate's head was bent over some papers on her desk, her lamp caught the amber highlights in her soft, glossy hair.

He knocked softly. Kate jumped. "I'm sorry to disturb you. I saw the light on."

"Don't tell me you're leaving before me. That's unheard of, Devlin." She looked at him curiously. "But it's Friday night, maybe you have a date..."

He walked into her office, its light feminine colors so different from his own corner office, and sat on a wing chair. Kate managed to hide her surprise at his uncharacteristic behavior. Uncharacteristic, hell, he and Ross had never even exchanged a few words on a personal level. He'd spent more time talking to her fiancé, Todd Miller. They'd even golfed together once or twice. He knew Miller to be a good guy—not one to abandon his responsibilities. It was Kate he didn't know very well. He'd only ever seen her as competition. It had been easier when he'd known nothing about her except her annoying traits. But his suspicions about her present situation made him want to reach out.

He realized he was perched awkwardly on the chair and leaned back.

Kate sat silently across from him, waiting. He'd always admired how she'd been able to wait out the opposition. Only now she was doing it to him. Again he noticed the circles under her eyes. Her figure, he knew, even hidden behind the mahogany desk, was trim and fit. No clues there, only nice feminine curves. He stopped himself from imagining Kate naked. He was her colleague, he reminded himself. He wanted to change the negative direction their association had taken. But he didn't know how and stumbled over his words. "If you're staying later than me, then you must be working too hard."

"No harder than you," she returned coldly. "Anderson hasn't made up his mind yet, has he?" She was suddenly suspicious. "Are you here to gloat?"

He winced. When had he and Ross turned this unpleasant toward each other?

"I was concerned about you today."

"Just a touch of the flu, Devlin. Nothing to keep me out of the race."

Devlin searched her desk, his eyes falling on her photos—one of her and Todd—smiling ecstatically at the camera. He might as well get straight to the point, small talk had never been his strong suit. "How is Todd? I haven't seen him around the office lately."

Kate stood and walked over to the window. She looked out and then turned toward him angrily. He noted how her hands protectively covered her stomach. At her action, his last doubt that his suspicions might be wrong fell away. When she noticed his eyes follow her movement, she dropped her hands to her sides, her fists clenched. "If you must know, Todd and I broke up several months ago. In fact, I haven't even spoken to him for a long while. So I have all of my time to devote to my career these days," she said. She tried but couldn't quite contain a note of bitterness.

"I hadn't heard. I'm sorry—"

"Nothing to be sorry about. We realized that marriage would have been a mistake. Is there anything else you wanted to know about my personal life?" She raised a haughty eyebrow.

"Er, no." He stood, uncomfortably aware that he was making a fool of himself. "Here. If you're staying late, you need to eat." He handed over Mrs. deVito's cannelloni, feeling like a Jewish mother. Bolting for the door, he mentally called himself every kind of idiot.

But that couldn't even begin to compare to the lunacy of what he planned to do next.

3

"WOULD YOU MIND telling me what this is about?" Todd Miller demanded as Devlin turned his Porsche onto the exit for Kate's address. Robert had always supposed that she lived in one of the exclusive condominiums along downtown Chicago's waterfront, and had been surprised to learn that her address was local.

Miller's question reminded Robert to stop analyzing the mysterious Kate Ross and concentrate on the situation between Kate and Miller. Despite the fact that Devlin had hauled Miller out of his Sunday-morning squash game, the man looked reasonably composed.

When Devlin had arrived at the Westport Health Club and announced that he needed Todd's help immediately, Todd had looked surprised but then made his excuses to his squash partner and left. Robert approved Todd's response—not asking questions until necessary, his willingness to help a casual acquaintance, without knowing that Kate was involved.

From his brief conversation with Kate on Friday, he had deduced that Todd did not know about the baby. But once Todd found out, Devlin was sure when he got Kate and Todd together, they'd solve their own problems. He could exit quickly and quietly and get back to his own life.

He could stop thinking about Kate. Stop noticing how pretty she was, even though she wasn't getting enough sleep. Stop considering all the ways he could help her, if only he had the right.

He had spent Saturday stewing over his discovery and what to do. At 5:00 a.m. Sunday morning, he'd decided that Todd had to know the truth, to face up to his responsibilities. Devlin had decided to track him down and drag him to Kate's condominium.

Devlin stopped his car in front of the address, a highrise in a nice residential neighborhood. "This is Kate's building," Miller said. He turned to Devlin, the questions he hadn't asked written on his handsome face. "Is something wrong?"

Devlin turned off the ignition. "In a manner of speaking, yes."

"And Kate sent *you* to get me?"

"No. I thought it was the best thing to do."

Shooting Devlin a very puzzled look, Miller got out of the car, entered the luxurious condominium building and waved at the elderly doorman, who greeted him by name and buzzed him through. Miller moved with athletic grace Robert noticed as Miller hurried ahead of him down the corridor. Kate was clearly attracted to blond, classical good looks in a man. Very different from what he looked like, Devlin reflected, and caught up with Todd at the elevators.

Kate had a corner unit on the seventh floor. Miller knocked loudly until they could hear footsteps. The door opened to reveal a thoroughly disheveled Kate— her hair in a sensuous mess around her face; a thin, very feminine, silky robe, which wasn't belted, thrown over her short nightgown; bare feet with pink-tipped toes. She had really sexy toes, Devlin realized. Todd surveyed her pleasant disarray and smiled.

"At least you haven't lost your fondness for sleeping late."

"Late, it's only nine-thirty!" Kate stood back from the door to let them in. Devlin wished she'd tie up her robe to cover her legs. They were even longer and shapelier than he'd imagined. "I'll go get some coffee," Kate said with a yawn and walked away. Devlin quashed his sudden feeling of jealousy that Kate wasn't surprised to see Miller at her door so early in the morning. Or that she hadn't seemed to notice him. This is exactly the situation he'd been hoping for, he reminded himself. Kate and Todd would resume their relationship.

Kate was halfway through her blue-and-white, country-style living room when complete awareness hit her and she stopped.

"What are you doing here?" Kate turned around slowly to stare at her early-morning intruders. Her hands touched her hair, trying to flatten the wild strands, but she only succeeded in messing it even more. Devlin suddenly wondered how often Miller had seen Kate's hair spread across the pillows, her familiar teasing smile on her face as she reached for him. At the rush of heat that spread through him, Devlin pushed away his ridiculous imaginings and surveyed the living room. The room was feminine, comfortable and a little messy—piles of magazines that weren't in the magazine rack, a stack of papers spread carelessly across an antique desk. To his surprise, close to the blue-and-white-striped couch, a pile of brightly colored yarns were falling out of a wicker basket. He frowned when he saw a half-finished baby booty on a knitting needle.

Determination made him square his shoulders. The little socks confirmed what he had already figured out. Todd Miller and Kate Ross had conceived a child.

Undoubtedly Miller and Kate had hit some kind of obstacle in their path to romantic happiness and split up. Kate, being proud and independent, would never use the baby to try to win Todd back. So her ex-fiancé had never been told.

Which was exactly the problem with modern relationships, Devlin thought. No one cared enough about family or stability to stay together long enough to work out their problems. And not hurt the children. Well, this was one child who would have two parents. He knew too much about broken families to not try to prevent another one.

Devlin returned his attention to Kate and Todd, but the pair were staring at each other with something like suspicion. Then Kate turned toward him and glared.

"What are *you* doing here?" she demanded. As if realizing her state of undress, and Robert's inability not to look at her, she blushed and pulled her robe together, tying it closed.

Todd interrupted the tension between Kate and Robert. "Devlin said it was an emergency. Kate, what's wrong?" Todd took her hands and pulled her protectively into an embrace.

Kate fitted easily under Todd's strong chin, her soft brown curls providing contrast to his straight blond hair. Devlin looked away, wondering where his pang of envy was coming from.

"There's nothing wrong with *me*," Kate answered in confusion, breaking away.

Devlin looked back at them as the two separated and stared at him expectantly. So much for hoping Kate would confess all as soon as she saw Todd.

It was up to him.

"Devlin." Kate took a step forward. For the first time ever, she looked concerned about him. She looked beautiful. "What is it?" she asked softly.

"It's the baby," he said baldly, and could have cursed himself for just spitting it out. But when Kate had looked at him as if she cared, he'd said the first words that popped into his head.

Kate gasped, her hand moving over her stomach.

Todd glared at Devlin. "What the hell are you talking about? Whose baby?"

"Kate's and yours." There, now he'd said it. He should leave and let the two of them work out their problems, but he found himself unable to move.

Todd grabbed Kate by the elbow and turned her to face him. "Is this true? Are you pregnant?"

Kate had paled. "Yes, but—"

"But I'm engaged." At Todd's words, Kate gasped again. Todd let go of her arm and looked around blindly.

Devlin felt a cold fury enter him. "Break the engagement. You have a prior responsibility with Ms. Ross."

"I can't." Miller looked like a man trapped as he ran a hand through his hair. He turned to Kate. "Kate, I love her—"

Devlin didn't know he was going to move until he'd knocked Todd down with a strong right hook. He grabbed Miller by the collar of his white country-club shirt and pulled him back to his feet. "You scum. You can't abandon Kate because you've found a new flavor of the month."

"Devlin!" Kate pulled at his arms. "Stop, please." The touch of her hands on him jerked him back to reality and he let go of Todd.

"I can't believe this," Kate fumed, her gaze raking the two of them. "Men!" She gave Devlin a look that told him she'd like to kill him slowly with her bare hands. "I'll get some ice for your eye, Todd. You—" she pointed at Devlin "—sit down and behave. I don't want to hear another word from either of you until I return."

Kate stomped out of the living room and through a swinging door to what he assumed was the kitchen. As he and Todd avoided each other's glances, Devlin heard the sound of an ice tray being angrily banged into the sink.

This wasn't going at all how he'd imagined. He couldn't believe any man would be such an idiot as to cheat on Kate.

She was back quickly and handed Todd an ice bag.

Kneeling down, she examined his eye, her hand stroking his cheek. "Oh, Todd..."

"Kate—" Todd took her hand with his free one "—why didn't you tell me?"

Kate sat back on her heels, disengaged her hand and glared at Devlin. "Because you're not the father. I'm three and a half months pregnant. We broke up more than six months ago," she added pointedly to Devlin.

"Oh." The relief on Miller's face was almost enough to make Devlin want to blacken his other eye. Did the man have no feelings for anyone other than himself? No wonder Kate had dumped him.

"But I don't understand, Kate. I haven't heard anything about a new man in your life," Todd said.

"Well, I hadn't heard anything about your new fiancée, either," Kate noted sourly, standing and moving away from him. She stared out of her large living-room window. Devlin saw her straighten her back, take a deep breath and turn to face Todd once again. "Although I'm really happy you found what you were looking for," she added genuinely. Her words were sincere, but Devlin noticed she had difficulty keeping eye contact with Todd.

"Yes, I'm very lucky to have found Lucy." Todd smiled warmly, the love for the new woman in his life written all over his face. Then he frowned, "But if I'm not the father of your baby, who is?"

Kate moved toward the ottoman and fingered the belt of her tightly tied robe. "It's no one you know."

"But does the man know he's about to be a father?" Devlin demanded. He might have made a mistake about Kate and Todd, but he could still help her. After this embarrassing morning, he *needed* to help her.

Kate turned on him. "What business is it of yours? What did you mean by dragging Todd over here? Were you going to use your caveman tactics and make him marry me?"

Devlin shifted uncomfortably under her furious gaze. "Yes."

That stopped everyone.

Suddenly the most gloriously radiant smile lit up Kate's face and Devlin felt a sharp, fierce heat spread through him. All of the pretend, courteous smiles she'd bestowed on him before faded into nothing next to the real thing. She shook her head, staring at him as if she'd never really seen him. "That's the sweetest, stupidest, most uptight thing I've ever heard. I always knew you were a straight arrow, Devlin, but this is beyond my wildest imaginings. Do-the-right-thing Devlin." She shook her head again, touching her stomach, as well. "Why are you doing this?"

"A child deserves to know his or her father."

Kate's eyes fell to her hands. She clasped and unclasped them, but remained silent.

"Devlin is right, Kate," Todd said gently. "You have to tell the father."

"I can't." She rose and began to pace the room. Robert had never seen her so upset and he blamed himself.

Todd, too, was agitated. "Oh, my God," he exclaimed, "don't tell me it was a one-night stand. I knew you weren't expecting our breakup, but I never thought you'd go off the deep end like that. Were you drunk? Do you even know his name?"

"No, I don't." Kate snapped. Her voice dripping with sarcasm, she asked, "If I give you a description, maybe my two he-man protectors can hunt him down and force him to the altar. Are either of you packing a magnum, because he was a rough character. A biker, I think—at least, he could open a beer bottle with his teeth."

She threw herself down on one of the overstuffed chairs and held a flowered cushion against her chest, taking a number of deep breaths. Devlin saw Todd open his mouth to speak, but Devlin shook his head to silence him.

"I am a thirty-six-year-old, successful, financially secure woman who is more than able to raise a child by herself," she said in what sounded to Devlin very much like a rehearsed speech. A niggling worry began in the back of his mind, but he refused to think about it. He was still too surprised to have learned that Todd broke up with Kate.

"Todd, you and Lucy have your own lives to lead now. I think it would be best if you left." When Devlin made a move, she fixed him with an ice-cold stare. "You, stay. We have a few matters to discuss."

Todd looked as if he wanted to protest, but wisely didn't. At the door, he leaned over and kissed Kate's cheek. "Call me if there's anything you need."

"I will. And Todd, I'm happy for you. About Lucy."

"You'd like her."

"I'm sure I would, but please don't invite me for brunch anytime too soon. My pride couldn't take it."

Kate closed the door behind Miller and leaned against it for a moment before moving toward Devlin. "How did you know?" she demanded. "Nobody except Jennifer knows."

"You were acting so differently, I knew something had to be...and then I put some clues together—your morning sickness, the soda crackers..." He trailed off.

"I'm working with a damn Columbo," she muttered. "Now what? When are you going to tell Larry Anderson?"

At his look of confusion, she snorted. "Oh, come on. For a puritan like Anderson, when you tell him about my...fall from grace, the promotion is yours."

"You don't really think I'm capable of that?"

"Then why were you snooping?"

"I wasn't snooping. I was concerned about you. I know you, Kate. When I thought Miller was the father, it seemed simple—get the two of you together—"

"And we'd do the right thing," Kate said with a sigh. Do-the-right-thing Devlin. "Why do you have such an obsession with my unborn child?"

"I don't." Devlin had no idea how to explain his concerns. Not without dragging his own messy past into the story. Why the idea of a child growing up without both a mother and a father hurt him. Kate wouldn't be interested. "I'd just like to help you, Kate."

She shook her head in wonder. "Do you realize you've never called me Kate before?"

"We've never really had a personal conversation be-fore."

"Well, next time we could have a conversation about the weather before segueing straight into my sex life."

"I'll remember that," Devlin said. Then, to his com-plete astonishment, he started to laugh.

Kate stared at him a moment, until she also began to chuckle. Then she laughed until the tears streamed down her face. She reached across the coffee table for a tissue and blew her nose. "Oh, this is the first good laugh I've had since I don't know when. Usually, I've gone through tissues because of my mood swings. And you know what the strangest thing of all is? I've never been so happy in my whole life."

Devlin rose. "Are you all right now?" At Kate's nod, he continued, "Then I think I should leave and let you enjoy your Sunday."

His hand was already on the doorknob when Kate asked in a very quiet voice, "Do you think Anderson will fire me?"

"No, he can't." Devlin whirled around. He imagined how senior management would take Kate's bombshell and felt sick. There had to be some way he could help her. Protect her.

Kate turned a very worried face to him. "Come on, Devlin, we both know senior management can do whatever they want—if they want to get rid of me, they'll find an excuse that has nothing to do with my pregnancy."

Devlin did his best to be reassuring, "Anderson and

his cronies are conservative, but I don't think they'll go that far. There will be a lot of questions, though."

"Yes." Kate sighed. "I've thought of that. I thought the truth...how much planning I've done for this baby...the nanny I've already hired..."

"Then you definitely will be having this child alone?" Devlin knew his tone was cold, but he couldn't approve of her actions. If anyone knew what it was like to be a kid without a complete family, it was him.

"Yes. You see, when Todd ended our engagement, it hurt, but I realized I was even more upset about not being able to begin a family." Kate took a deep breath and stopped shredding the tissue in her hands. "So I decided to have a child."

"So you went out and seduced a man?" Devlin asked, sending up a silent prayer that the answer would be yes. *Please let it be yes.*

"No, I couldn't do that. I didn't want to trick anyone."

Devlin closed his eyes and prayed one more time she wouldn't say—

"I went to a sperm bank."

4

"OF COURSE, it's just a coincidence," Devlin said to Alan Blackwood, and took a swig of his lemonade. He'd have preferred a beer, but he was taking Philip, Alan's five-year-old son and his godson, to the park. Betty and Alan were expecting their second child in a few weeks and Robert knew they could use a few hours alone.

Besides, he enjoyed his monthly afternoons with Philip. Although he couldn't begin to answer all of the boy's questions or keep up with his energy. Still, Robert felt comfortable with the Blackwoods, like part of their family in a slightly removed fashion. He knew that deep down Betty would like nothing better than to set him up with one of her girlfriends, but after ten years of him declining all such invitations she had given up.

No, the way he had his life set up was the best. The occasional woman for...companionship, and the Blackwoods as a family he could visit whenever he wanted. He treasured the time he spent with them and therefore made sure he limited how often he saw them. So that he wouldn't be a burden. So that he wouldn't annoy them and ruin something he cared about.

Alan shook his head. "It is definitely a coincidence.

The odds have to be about a billion to one. Come on."
Alan slapped him on the shoulder. "You did a good
deed—hell, a noble deed. Without someone like you,
Betty and I wouldn't have Philip."

Suddenly, a blond-haired dervish charged into the
kitchen and threw himself into Robert's lap. "Uncle
Rob, Uncle Rob. I've been waiting for you *forever*. Can
we go now?"

Philip Harris Blackwood leaped onto the floor,
thrust his arms out and began to vroom like a plane.
The boy's fair coloring was from Betty. Physically there
was nothing of Alan, of course, but Robert saw the
family connection in their mannerisms, in the love between father and son.

That was what being a family was all about. The
time he spent with the Blackwoods always reaffirmed
his decision not to marry and have a family of his own.

After his mother had abandoned him when he was
seven, Robert had spent the rest of his childhood in a
series of foster homes, each one worse than the last.
Shortsighted, with thick lenses, small for his age and
afraid that his foster parents would leave him, Robert
had determinedly remained a loner. No one would
ever be able to hurt him again, the way his mother had.

His mother had always told him in no uncertain
terms that she resented him because his existence had
driven away his father.

Today Robert understood that the surly, unattractive
boy who shunned any attempt at friendliness had been
too much of a misfit. That prospective adoptive parents
naturally chose the other children. But it had always

hurt, no matter how much he had pretended it didn't. Moreover, his childhood scars had stayed with him. He knew that he held some kind of flaw, that while no longer visible to the eye was still there. He was incapable of forming lasting relationships. In thirty-eight years, no one had ever loved him.

He wouldn't have even minded being scorned in love. Experienced unrequited love. But he'd never experienced it at all. He'd tried. He'd dated very nice, likable, suitable women. He'd felt passion for them. Lust. But never once had he felt love.

Clearly, some people were incapable and he was one of them. He'd gotten used to it.

And he'd learned to accept his own limitations. That some people could never be comfortable or wanted in a close-knit group like a family. That it was better to be an occasional welcome visitor than an unwanted hanger-on.

He didn't fit in. He made people uncomfortable. So he'd learned to demand absolutely nothing. To keep an emotional distance in order not to be rejected.

Instead, he threw all his emotions and passion into work. For him, Carlyle Industries was his family.

Alan Blackwood was the only exception.

Somehow they had become and remained friends. At first, Robert had worried, wondering when the friendship would change, when Alan would see him for the flawed individual he knew he was, but it hadn't occurred.

Robert had had casual friends and relationships throughout college. It was when he'd been studying for his master's in business that he'd met Alan. They'd shared a bathroom on the grad students' floor and had become study partners. Each had been determined to do well, to graduate at the top of their respective classes. And they had. Their friendly rivalry had spurred each to work harder.

They'd also had a lot of time to talk. Alan learned all about Devlin; in fact, he knew him better than anyone did. Robert had expected their friendship to decline into a pleasant memory after graduation, but as they'd both found jobs in Chicago, it had continued.

When Alan had fallen in love with Betty and then married her, Robert had expected to lose his friend. To his disbelief, the pair had welcomed him into their family and made him godfather of their firstborn.

He'd spent a lot of Friday nights at their home, enjoying their family life, discussing Alan's law practice, Betty's patients. Alan planned to practice corporate law for several years and then open a small firm of his own. Betty was a nurse and Robert knew she was a natural caregiver. For whatever reason, Alan and Betty had made him part of their family. A family that the couple had frequently talked about increasing.

Devlin had known that the Blackwoods had had difficulty conceiving the first time, but it wasn't until Betty became pregnant a second time that Alan had confided about the problem. Alan had been so overjoyed at the news of his wife's pregnancy that he and Robert had shared a few beers too many at their favorite watering hole. Alan had revealed that his low sperm count had been the culprit and that he and Betty had used a sperm bank for both pregnancies. Alan said he didn't know what they would have done without modern medicine.

Robert had been stunned. Having decided that he would never have a family of his own because no woman would ever stay with him for long, he realized he could help others in the same predicament as the Blackwoods. He'd gone to the clinic the Blackwoods had used and made a donation.

When he'd told Alan what he'd done, Alan had hugged him and thanked him. And they'd never spoken of it again.

"Vroom." Philip flew in front of Robert and looked at him expectantly.

Robert felt a familiar pull on his heart as he looked at the little boy's happy face. "Where are your shoes?" he asked. "We can't go anywhere without your shoes."

As Philip ran off in search of the elusive footwear, Alan smiled. "Don't worry, Devlin. You did the right thing."

KATE WATCHED Ellen Chase scribble something in illegible doctorese into her medical file. Ellen closed the file and leaned back in her chair, smiling. "You're in excellent health and the baby is doing well. At your next visit, which will be the end of the second trimester, we'll begin to schedule biweekly visits. Have you begun childbirth classes yet?"

Alarmed, Kate paled. "No, I've been very busy. Is there some reason I should have started already? Are you expecting the baby early?"

Ellen shook her head, her fine brunette hair moving softly around her face. "No, no, Kate. You're fine, the baby is fine. I'm only concerned about you as a friend. How are you handling everything? Your family? Work?" Her clear blue eyes examined Kate.

Kate twisted the strap of her purse in her hands. "Not as well as I'd imagined." She sighed, trying to put into words all her contradictory emotions. Not to mention the bizarre incident with Devlin. The man had been intruding more and more on her thoughts ever since. "I'm distracted. I've really fallen behind in my work."

"You can't expect to do everything. The media's image of women being able to do it all is pure fantasy. And insidious when society expects you to do just that. How did your parents take the news?"

"They don't know yet. They're really busy with their move from Chatham to Chicago, so we've only spoken on the phone," Kate admitted miserably. "I know I'm being a coward, but until I really start to show, I'm putting off the announcement. Now everyone at the office is convinced I'm turning into a real tubbo." Kate took a deep breath. "I'm going to tell my folks this weekend, when I go home to visit them." That should be interesting. "Telling the people at work I want to delay until the last possible minute." That would be even more...interesting.

Ellen grinned. "I can understand. Just remember not to push yourself too hard. At least you have Jennifer."

"And Devlin." Kate was surprised she'd admitted

this to Ellen, or that she really did consider Devlin to be on her side.

"Robert Devlin? The evil I'll-do-anything-to-win Devlin?"

Kate shifted uncomfortably. "I may have exaggerated when I described him. He figured out I was pregnant and, well, he's been really decent about it. In fact, he even covered for me once when I had to miss a meeting to see you. That's why I appreciate your squeezing me in on a Saturday morning."

Casual friends, Kate was grateful that Ellen had been willing to be her doctor. It was knowing Ellen worked at a fertility clinic that had helped Kate make her decision. Ellen had been so giving with her time and information and so concerned for her.

Which made her present feelings even worse. Being pregnant—being *single* and pregnant—was more than she'd ever imagined. Yes, the rewards, the wonder overrode her worries. But not knowing who the father was had begun to disturb her profoundly.

It wasn't Devlin's ravings over the father's right to know—the man who had donated his sperm to the clinic had willingly accepted this fact—but her child's inevitable questions that plagued her. At Christmas, when Kate joined her relatives at her parents' house, and her child, looking at the mummies and daddies gathered around the table, asked who her father was, Kate could hardly point to the turkey baster.

There was just something in her that demanded to know. She needed to know who the father was, what kind of man he was, so she could tell her child.

Ridiculous, Kate firmly told herself. There was no way to find out.

The impossible had never stopped her before, she reminded herself.

It would be unethical to break into the man's privacy, her conscience said.

Why? Kate demanded. She wouldn't do anything about it. She just needed to know. It would be better for the baby if she knew.

Kate rose as Ellen stood and moved around the desk to hug her. "Thank you so much for everything, Ellen. I couldn't have done this without you." She hugged Ellen again and, at the same time, reached down to the desk and flipped open her chart. Scanning its contents, she found her patient number: 541.

Thanking Ellen once more, Kate left the plainly decorated office, exited through the waiting room, which held two very pregnant women, and made her way out.

She wondered if she dared do what she was considering.

Was she really going to break the rules again? Sure, that approach worked for her in her career, even at Carlyle, which was so stuck in its ways, but what she was planning was much bigger. She was considering ignoring the regulations that protected anonymous donors to the sperm bank.

Hang the rules. She needed to know. For her baby's future.

Lost in thought, Kate barely glanced at her surroundings as she stepped outside. The sunlight was bright and she stopped at the bottom steps to put on her sunglasses.

"Ms. Ross," a familiar voice said. A voice that had spent too much time in her thoughts recently.

Kate looked up in surprise. Robert Devlin and a young boy were standing in front of her. "Devlin," she managed to say. For some reason, she felt acutely uncomfortable with him, here, in front of the clinic. It was just coincidence that he was walking by.

"Hi," the boy said curiously.

"Philip, this is Ms. Ross. We work together," Devlin said, taking hold of the boy's hand when he looked as if he was about to run up the steps into the clinic. "This is my godson, Philip Blackwood."

"This is where I was born," Philip announced proudly. "My sister is gonna be born here, too."

"You were born at the hospital, the doctors at this clinic helped," Devlin corrected gently. He looked at Kate carefully, his gaze falling to her growing stomach. She was showing a little, but he hadn't heard any gossip at work about her condition. Kate had good relationships among most of the female employees and the men had probably only noticed Kate's new, lush figure. He had. Too often he found himself imagining what she looked like under her business suit.

Lost in his images, he suddenly realized that Kate was waiting for him to explain. "Philip's parents told him about the fertility clinic, especially since he has a little sister on the way and his mother had to try several times...he doesn't understand all of it, naturally."

"He's a lovely boy." They stood uncomfortably for a

few seconds as Devlin looked at her, at Philip and then at the clinic. "Is this where...?"

"Yes. Dr. Chase is a friend of mine and it seemed to make sense..." She trailed off, noticing Devlin had grown very pale.

"You're five months?" he asked as if he was calculating something.

"Yes."

"Oh... Well." He took off his glasses, folded them closed, then opened them and put them on again. With his peculiar distracted air, Kate thought he looked much more approachable than at the office. Do-the-right-thing Devlin seemed so much more...human. The fact that the little blond boy was gazing at him with adoration also helped gentle Devlin's usually harsh features. She was beginning to see why some of the women at Carlyle considered Devlin sexy.

She shook herself. Sexy! Clearly her hormones were working overtime.

"Philip and I were in the park and he likes to come by here," Devlin explained.

"Uncle Rob, you promised ice cream." Philip tugged on Devlin's hand.

Devlin smiled at the boy and Kate was struck by the obvious love between the two. She had clearly underestimated coldhearted Devlin.

"We'd better go," he said. "I'll see you at work on Monday."

"Sure, I'll send over some inflated numbers that you can slash." Devlin didn't smile—she'd been wishing he would. Instead, he nodded and the pair walked off,

Philip beginning what appeared to be a very important conversation, judging by how close Devlin leaned in toward the little boy. Devlin pointed, seeming to explain something.

She realized her child wouldn't have a man like Devlin to explain things.

Kate stared after them until the two reached the corner and Devlin turned around and stared at the clinic. He shook his head and then noticed that Kate was still standing on the street watching him and Philip.

Across the fifty yards, their gazes locked and Kate felt frozen to the spot. Impossibly, she felt...*connected* to Devlin and couldn't break the moment. Neither, it seemed, could he—not until Philip pulled on his godfather's arm and Devlin turned away to kneel next to the boy.

Unsettled, Kate turned around and hurried toward her car.

Hormones! Pregnant women were subject to mood swings because of all the body's changes, Kate knew. She'd been reading up.

It was only hormones.

"NOW PANT," the instructor said, and Kate panted.

Jennifer rubbed Kate's shoulders as the childbirth leader had already shown them.

In the class of ten couples, Kate was glad there was another pair of women like herself and Jennifer. The male-female couple thing got to her sometimes when she was surrounded by happy pregnant women.

"Take that silly grin off your face," Kate said between pants.

Jennifer giggled.

"No giggling, either!"

"Sorry, but you just don't look like the vice president of Marketing, North America, right now."

Kate gave out a grunt and glared at Jennifer, who, even dressed in sweats, still managed to look like a vice president. She wondered where Jennifer bought tailored sweat suits and wished they came in maternity sizes. Kate just looked fat in her oversize T-shirt and leggings. She wished she could smoothly jump to her feet and smack Jennifer, the way she could have before, but her no-longer svelte—okay, large—girth didn't allow it. "I don't have the job yet, and the way I'm going, I won't. That's why I need to get rid of distractions—to concentrate on the baby and the promotion. Find out who the father is, then put it out of my mind."

She wasn't going to be part of a happy couple like so many of her classmates were, but at least she could tell her child about her father. Kate had decided she was going to have a girl. She'd decided, she hadn't asked. That was one aspect of her pregnancy she wanted to do the old-fashioned way.

The childbirth instructor started demonstrating another massage technique. Under her breath, Jennifer began to list her objections. "First, what you're suggesting is illegal. What would happen to your precious promotion if we got caught? Second, look at these couples, half of them will be divorced before the kid is

ten." Kate winced at Jennifer's bitterness. "You're better off doing this alone. Third, how could we do it?"

Deciding to leave the topic of happy marriages
alone, Kate revealed her plan. "I helped Ellen with the
clinic's computer system. The key was my patient
number. Now that I have it, the two of us could crack
the system easy."

"Four," Jennifer continued smoothly as if she hadn't
heard a word Kate had said, "what would you do with
the information? Track him down and make him be a
part of your life? Mr. X donated his sperm so that you
could have a healthy baby without involving him. It
would be like a breach of promise."

Kate shifted over to her side and began her contraction exercises. "Of course I wouldn't interfere in his
life. I'd never tell him. But I need to know."

Jennifer sat back on her heels, letting Kate work
alone for a minute. "The rules exist for a reason, Kate.
You're too used to doing everything your own way."

Kate knew that Jennifer was right, but she didn't
know how to explain the need within her. It gnawed at
her day and night. Until she found out the answer, she
wouldn't be able to think of anything else and that
couldn't be good for the baby, she rationalized.

But she couldn't tell Jennifer that. Instead, she fell
upon the weak but only argument she could come up
with. "What if my kid is really good with her hands? If
the father is a carpenter then I'll know her skill is inherited and I should encourage it. I don't want to hold
back my own kid because of unconscious sexual prej-
udices."

"And if the father is a ruthless corporate executive?"

"Then I'll insist she take liberal arts before sending her to Harvard for her MBA. For a well-rounded education."

Jennifer shook her head but then smiled at Kate. "This is the stupidest idea you've ever had."

"THIS IS THE STUPIDEST IDEA you've ever had," Jennifer whispered as she hit another computer key. "Hold that flashlight higher, I can barely see the keyboard."

Kate raised the light. "Hurry," she said, and glanced nervously around the empty waiting room of the clinic. It was dark except for the small amount of light she was holding over Jennifer's head. For about an hour she and Jennifer had been working together at Ellen's PC, trying to break her codes. Because she knew Ellen, it had been a fairly simple task to figure out her password. After running through her birthday, the names of her children and husband, it had turned out to be the name of Ellen's college boyfriend.

Getting into the office had been fairly easy, as well. Kate had simply scheduled her appointment as the last one of the day and then, rather than leaving the building, had hidden in a closet until everyone left. She'd remained in her uncomfortable location for another two hours until the cleaning staff had also come and gone. All the time she'd talked to her unborn daughter, assuring her that her mother was doing the right thing. That they wouldn't be caught and she wouldn't be sent to jail.

Kate hadn't known she would be so scared. Scared at

the idea of being caught. Scared by what she would soon learn.

Once again, she told herself she was doing the right thing.

She was.

She'd finally left her hiding spot at nine to wait for Jennifer. At nine-thirty she'd let Jennifer into the building and since then they'd been making steady progress with the computer.

"Okay," Jennifer said triumphantly. "In the file of patient 541, the sperm donor was number 2-C-A1."

"You make it sound so cold," Kate joked, trying to insert some humor into the situation. She wiped her sweaty palms against her thighs. It wasn't too late to turn back. She could tell Jennifer that they should leave. That everyone else and their rules were right, and she was wrong.

She opened her mouth and then shut it. She wasn't a coward. And she really needed to know the answer.

Jennifer didn't acknowledge Kate's lame attempt at levity, but continued to work. She cross-referenced files and then typed in 2-C-A1. She held her finger over the enter key. "Are you sure?"

Kate took a deep breath. What she was doing was wrong, but she just had to know. "Yes." She closed her eyes and said a little prayer. She wasn't sure for what.

Opening her eyes, she saw Jennifer's shocked face. Jennifer's mouth was moving but no sound came out.

With a sense of inevitability, Kate peered over Jennifer's shoulder to read the name of her baby's father.

The name seemed to glow mockingly at her on the computer screen.

Robert Devlin.

5

"IT'S GRANNIE GOODSPOON." Jennifer blurted out the words as she raced into Kate's office.

Kate blanched. The reference to the baby-food company reminded her of her own baby. She'd barely slept in the last two nights, hardly able to believe that Robert Devlin was the father of her child. No wonder he'd looked so shocked when he'd run into her outside the fertility clinic.

But why had coldhearted Devlin involved himself with a fertility clinic? Out of the goodness of his heart? To help some hopeful, desperate couple become parents? Hardly, she snorted to herself. More likely it was part of the old-boys' network—a way to make points in the corporate boardroom. Well, wait until they found out she'd beaten them all!

Kate realized she was becoming hysterical and shook her head. Ever since she'd learned the awful truth—the truth that she'd been so determined to know—she hadn't been able to think clearly.

Oh, if only she'd listened to Jennifer and not found out who the father of her baby was.

She had absolutely no idea what she was going to do. As long as the man had been a stranger, she'd assumed she could learn a few things about him—without his knowledge—and leave it at that.

But it was Robert Devlin. A man who, until two months ago, she had more or less hated.

They were having a baby! Together!

Considering how he had dragged Todd to her home to marry her because of the baby, she wondered if she should tell Robert the truth.

No, that was the worst idea she'd had yet. For once, she would follow the rules. Robert Devlin had been promised anonymity by the clinic and she wasn't going to do anything more toward breaking that promise. She wasn't.

"What?" Jennifer asked.

"What, what?"

"You made a funny noise. Are you feeling sick?" Jennifer grabbed the wastepaper basket and offered it to Kate.

"No, no. I was just thinking about..." The two friends remained silent; they hadn't spoken a word about what they'd learned.

Kate was grateful that Jennifer had restrained herself from saying "I told you so." As usual, she had followed her gut instincts as opposed to cool logic. It was so like her to just go barreling forward. No thought for the consequences but full speed ahead. Now look at the mess she was in.

Why couldn't she have respected the rules? The rules she had promised not to break. Oh no, she had to do everything her way. The rules weren't meant for her.

Wasn't that what drove Robert Devlin crazy about her? Her arrogant insistence that she could do it her way. Her lack of respect for organization, structure, rules.

"Grannie Goodspoon," Jennifer reminded Kate.

Jennifer sounded panicky. Grannie Goodspoon was Carlyle Industries' biggest competitor in the food sector. But Carlyle planned to increase their market share with their new line of baby-food products. Kate was extremely proud of their baby food. The From Mother's Kitchen products stressed quality and natural ingredients. The marketing campaign, which she had been in charge of, would be rolling out onto TV, radio and magazines in six months. The same time that From Mother's Kitchen Baby Foods would be on the supermarket shelves.

"Grannie's Baby Food will be in the stores in three months," Jennifer announced baldly, a tiny bead of sweat over her upper lip.

Kate felt sick. It couldn't be true. "What? They didn't even have a plan for baby food last month." Kate didn't believe this was happening. How the devil had Goodspoon created a product without anyone at Carlyle hearing a word? Damn and double damn. If it was true, it was the third time in four years that Goodspoon had bested them. But the other times, it had been a fair race. Goodspoon hadn't been able to join in near the finish line like now.

"Benson was having dinner with our central manufacturers when one of them let it slip about the new account with Grannie Goodspoon," Jennifer told her.

"Anderson's called an emergency executive meeting. Starting now."

"Damn," Kate said. She looked around her office wondering if she should grab a file or something, but her files didn't hold any of the answers. First, the father of her baby turned out to be Robert Devlin and, now, her most important assignment at Carlyle Industries, the baby-food line, was being preempted by Grannie Goodspoon. What in the world could go wrong next? Jennifer nodded toward the hallway and Kate shrugged. "Let's go," she agreed, and they hurried down the plush, carpeted hallway to the boardroom.

At its solid oak-paneled door, Kate paused and held a hand to her stomach, but it wasn't because of the baby. Dread, imminent doom, plain old-fashioned fear was making her stomach knot. From Mother's Kitchen was her project. Big trouble. She should have found out about Goodspoon's new product line before Benson.

She was afraid that the unlucky third thing that would happen to her—her mother said that bad news always came in threes—would be Anderson's announcement that Devlin had the promotion.

And after this huge mistake on her part, she'd have to agree that Anderson had made the right decision. Taking a deep breath, she walked in the room like the lamb to the slaughter.

Devlin looked up from his perfectly centered portfolio and glasses. Their eyes met and the expression he saw in hers was one of...fright. Confused, he grabbed his glasses, but by the time he had them on, Kate had settled into her chair across the table from him. He saw her put on her professional, nothing-can-stop-me face as she nodded at Benson and Diamente. In all the dark wood, subdued upholstery and pin-striped suits, her red-and-white combination stood out. The long red jacket was buttoned over the knit winter-white dress. He knew very well how that dress hugged her curves and had once lost himself for several minutes in a meeting staring at the long expanse of thigh the side slit of the dress exposed.

Still, he was all too aware that her jacket was buttoned to cover her growing middle. He'd always considered the peacock colors she wore blatant attention-grabbing. But he was having to reconsider. Any woman who decided to have a child by herself because she wanted so much to be a mother wasn't doing it for the attention; it was because of her independent streak. She wasn't anything like his own mother. Kate really didn't give a damn what others thought. She dressed not to fit in as he did, but to please herself.

Belonging was so much easier for her.

Despite her bright colors, her determined face, Devlin could see the dark smudges beneath her eyes, lines of worry around her mouth. Was it the pregnancy or something else that was troubling Kate Ross? She caught him staring at her and dropped her gaze to her fidgeting hands.

Benson leaned toward Kate and said something Robert couldn't hear. Kate stiffened, but in a calm voice she said, "On the contrary, I'm thankful you did find out about Grannie Goodspoon's campaign. Now we can work together to speed up production and get into the marketplace first.'' The flinty gaze she turned on Benson made the man keep his mouth shut.

Devlin smiled at her. Kate's eyes widened in surprise, but then she smiled back. For one second they were united, until Kate looked away. Devlin wished she would have continued to smile at him like that. He mentally shook himself and told himself to stop dreaming like a love-struck adolescent.

He'd been spending far too much time thinking about Kate Ross. Ever since he'd learned that she was no longer engaged to Miller, he couldn't stop thinking of her as a woman. No longer was she the corporate competitor, an adversary he despised. Instead, he would daydream about her sparkling blue eyes, her soft hair, her lips…

He was worse than a teenager. Devlin decided to put this nonsense behind him. He'd felt desire for female colleagues and each time he had quelled the feelings. He would do the same now.

But he'd never had the desire to protect a woman before.

Larry Anderson strode in and took his position at the head of the table. A big man with dark hair and a jovial exterior, he fooled some people into believing he couldn't make ruthless decisions; Devlin and everyone in the room knew better. He could fire an employee of many years without losing his smile. But he also rewarded hard work; it was because of him that Carlyle had increased its market share so dramatically over the last decade.

Anderson picked up his gold pen and began to nervously tap it against the table. Having recently given up smoking, Anderson fiddled.

"I'm sure all of you have heard the news by now." He solemnly surveyed his management team: Silver, Benson, Givens, Diamente, Ross, Lockwood, Swinson from Finance, Lipp, the head of production. "Somehow, Grannie Goodspoon learned of our new product launch, created their own replica and are going to beat us onto the supermarket shelves by three months."

Lipp spoke. "What they've accomplished—creating, testing a new line of baby foods—is impossible."

"They've done it," Benson insisted. "My distributors weren't lying."

"I'm not insinuating they were," Lipp continued. He was a good man to have when there was trouble—cool and clear-thinking. Carlyle Industries couldn't have asked for a better man in charge of production. Emergencies were just another day at work to him. "What I'm saying is that it should be impossible."

"But they have done it," Devlin said, understanding what Lipp meant.

"Exactly." Lipp nodded and stayed silent.

"Oh." Kate gasped as she, too, realized Lipp's point. Jennifer paled slightly, while Diamente frowned.

"What?" Benson demanded. "What is it?"

"The only way Grannie Goodspoon could have accomplished so much so quickly was if they had inside information," Devlin clarified, while hardly able to believe his own words.

"If they were stealing from us," Jennifer added bleakly.

Damn, Devlin thought. That meant that someone high up was leaking extremely confidential information to good old Grannie. It could be any of them or any one of their assistants. He felt personally betrayed that someone in Carlyle could behave in such an underhand manner and vowed to do whatever it took to find the culprit.

"It's even worse." Anderson broke the heavy silence, his voice cold with disapproval. "Goodspoon also knows our marketing campaign. They're calling their baby-food line From Grannie's Kitchen."

Kate flushed with outrage. That was a direct rip-off! How could this have happened? Didn't the Goodspoon company have any integrity? Competition was one thing, but stealing... She realized the whole table was looking at her, waiting for her to speak. Jennifer studied her with support written all over her face, Lipp neutral, as always, Diamente and Silver puzzled, Benson pleased at her predicament, Devlin...unreadable. His strong face remained unmoving, his mouth a straight line, his eyes watching her. Surely he had to know that she could never betray Carlyle.

"Kate?" Anderson broke into her churning thoughts. His jovial mask was dropped, the steely businessman apparent. "This was your project. Can you enlighten us on how this could have happened?"

Kate folded her hands in her lap and took a deep breath to quell her rising panic. This couldn't be happening to her. Now...at the very worst and best time of her life. She'd been relying upon the successful launch of From Mother's Kitchen Baby Foods to act as her insurance policy for when she made her own baby announcement.

A baby in the boardroom would only be tolerated as long as she excelled. Instead, disaster was staring her in the face.

"I don't know," she admitted. "Until Benson made his startling discovery, neither I nor any member of my group were aware of any competition from Goodspoon."

"But where could they have gotten our product-development and marketing plans from?" Devlin asked.

Was he accusing her? Kate wondered. She'd been expecting the attack from Benson and Silver, not Devlin.

Why not? her conscience chided. She and Devlin were the front-runners for the job the whole group coveted. A fall like this was exactly what she'd been wishing on him.

She raised her chin and opened her mouth. At first, no sound came out, but then in a firm voice she said, "Devlin is right. Where could the leak have happened except in my department? I take full responsibility."

"That's not what I meant," he exclaimed angrily and took off his glasses. Kate was intrigued by how dark his brown eyes became when he was angry.

He turned toward Anderson. "Kate would never do anything to hurt Carlyle."

"It's her department. Her responsibility." Silver quickly joined in on the attack.

Devlin glared at him. "The leak could have come from any department."

"Agreed," Jennifer added in her calm voice. "We need to decide what to do now. Do we go ahead or stop our campaign?"

Lipp frowned at some papers in front of him and then sighed. "I could get From Mother's Kitchen onto the market in three months."

"On the exact launch date as Grannie Goodspoon?" Kate asked, feeling the first glimmer of hope.

"Yes."

As one unit, they all relaxed. If Arthur Lipp said he could do something, he did it.

"But if Goodspoon learns what we're doing, could they speed up their launch date?"

"No." This time Devlin answered. He put his glasses back on and made sure they sat properly, back in full control of himself. "I know the production manager at Goodspoon. He's always complained how lean his staff is—how deadlines are constantly missed. If they've stolen our plans, they won't be able to react to a change in our plans."

Kate hoped they couldn't. Carlyle had to enter the market at the same time as Goodspoon. It was their only chance if they were going to duke it out in the kitchen with Grannie. Mixing spoons at twenty paces—Kate couldn't help smiling at the image.

"This is no laughing matter, Ross," Anderson stated.

"Oh, no. It was just...nerves," Kate replied, and knew she'd said the wrong thing. The only nerves Carlyle executives were permitted to have were nerves of steel.

Anderson continued to stare disapprovingly, but Kate had learned. She faced him unmoving, waiting for his pronouncement.

"Well, then..." Anderson continued to study her and then his gaze rested on the others briefly. At Devlin, something twitched in his face but Kate couldn't tell what emotion he was hiding.

And then she knew. It was pleasure. Oh, God, Anderson was going to give her project to Devlin. Do-the-right-thing Devlin would save the day. Then he'd become vice president, Marketing.

And she'd be...a mother.

Kate closed her eyes. The baby kicked and she let her hands drift to her stomach. She didn't need maternity clothes yet, she was wearing whatever stretched. Despite all the books she'd read, she was still amazed at the changes her body was going through.

Suddenly, she opened her eyes. Okay, so Devlin was going to win. He'd be the vice president.

She even had to admit he'd probably make a good vice president.

She, however, was going to be a mother.

Kate smiled at Anderson.

"Good, Ms. Ross." Anderson's voice was hard. "I'm glad to see you've recovered so quickly. Making plans for the next step?"

Was she ever, Kate thought. She could paint bunnies onto the nursery walls this weekend. And maybe pick out a crib. Call her sister Anne and get together for lunch. Anne would be able to give her all sorts of advice about babies.

"Because I find failure unacceptable," Anderson said. "You'll need all of your energy as you head up the emergency team to solve this crisis. I want our baby food in the stores at the same time as Goodspoon's line. Except consumers will be picking our brand because of our unique marketing pitch."

Kate swallowed. *Unique marketing pitch.*

Forget the bunnies—she'd be working even harder. She couldn't manage to contain her surprise that she was still in charge. "Yes," she managed to say, "I'll get it done."

Anderson looked pleased with himself. "Don't worry, Ms. Ross, you'll have some help. Devlin will be your partner. You two will be the coheads of the project. I expect my fiercest competitors to work together to face Carlyle Industries' darkest day."

Oh, my! Kate thought. Work together...

Long hours and nights spent with the man who had fathered her child. A man she was increasingly attracted to. A man who was her ruthless adversary.

"In the meantime," Anderson continued smoothly, ignoring the shock on Devlin's face and what had to be shock on her own, "I am going to conduct an investigation into who is our corporate spy."

He glared at all of them. "And when I find out who has been leaking information to Grannie—" He gestured a slice across the throat that would have made any mafia boss proud.

Kate shivered. Anderson's threat wasn't anywhere near as disturbing as the thought of working side by side with Robert Devlin.

6

SHE WAS SO TIRED. Kate raised her arms, trying to stretch out the knots in her shoulders. Then she picked up the revised production printouts Devlin had left on her desk and initialed her approvals. She and Devlin had so many areas to cover that they had divided the work into two. For the past week, their only means of communication had been electronic mail and voice mail.

Nor was the atmosphere at Carlyle any help. Tempers flared and everyone was suspicious of everyone else. She'd seen Benson and Silver almost come to blows, until Devlin stepped in. Even she had taken to locking her important documents in her briefcase and taking them home at night. She sighed. Yes, her briefcase was sharing her bed with her these days. She refused to remember who she had dreamed about sharing her bed with last night. This pregnancy was clearly making her a little nuts.

The important fact to keep in mind was that someone at Carlyle was betraying them. The only person she trusted implicitly was Jennifer. And Devlin. That was funny; but the more she learned about him, the more she realized that Devlin cared about Carlyle, almost like a family. He would never betray an institution he loved.

She also knew that he would feel betrayed if she ever told him the truth about the baby. Whatever his reasons for participating with the fertility clinic, Devlin clearly believed he'd be helping a couple. He would be horrified to learn that she was the mother of his child.

Tonight was the first time she'd lain eyes on him since the emergency executive meeting. But all he'd done was wander in and hand over his analysis. She'd opened her mouth to ask him to stay, then stopped herself. She and Devlin had nothing in common to talk about.

That she had dreamed about him for three nights in a row was only because she knew...

She didn't like Robert Devlin, she firmly told herself, knowing she was lying.

Outside in the hallway Kate heard Devlin's low voice and a woman's answer. She couldn't overhear the words, but the woman's tone was animated. Even Devlin sounded more human.

Kate decided she needed a reference book from one of the shelves across the room. She walked over and flipped through the pages, glancing casually down the hall through the open door.

The woman, a vivacious brunette, arched her neck and laughed. Devlin smiled and touched her arm. Gina King. Kate recognized the woman as Benson's secretary. As Kate watched, Gina looked around the empty corridor and then reached up to kiss Devlin on the mouth. Oh, it was a quick chaste kiss, but it was *on the mouth.*

The book snapped shut in Kate's hands, but neither Gina nor Robert seemed to hear.

"Thanks, Robert," Gina said. "I'll see you Saturday." Devlin watched her walk away and Kate imagined him smiling again. Then he turned around and saw Kate.

He blushed. He actually blushed, Kate realized. Robert Devlin and Gina King. She never would have imagined them as a couple. Gina had such a zest for life while Devlin ran his life according to rigid schedules. Kate was also shocked that do-the-right-thing Devlin was involved with someone at work.

Devlin shrugged uncomfortably. "It's not—"

Kate interrupted him, not wanting to hear any explanations, "It's none of my business," Kate said. And she closed her office door.

She had to lean against the solid wood to catch her breath as she wondered what other secrets Devlin was hiding. One kiss was not a clandestine affair, she told herself firmly. It didn't have to mean anything. It certainly didn't mean that Robert was guilty of anything.

But she wished he'd been kissing her.

ON SUNDAY MORNING, Kate heard a furious pounding on her door. She threw back her downy comforter, put her feet on the floor, stretched and considered whether she needed to go to the bathroom to throw up. No, she decided, her morning sickness, which had lasted much longer than the first trimester, finally seemed to be over.

She grabbed a white Victorian-lace robe trimmed with blue, and put it on as she went to answer the door. Kate realized she was smiling and tried to stop, but she couldn't. Joe the doorman—as sweet as the old man was—had one fault: once he'd let someone up unannounced, he continued to do so. The elderly man was also a romantic and seemed to believe that well-dressed, attractive gentleman callers should be encouraged.

Which meant her early-morning visitor had to be— "Morning, Devlin," she said as she opened the door. Why was she so happy that he was here?

"You should check who it is before you let me in," he grumbled.

She headed back toward the living room and waved at a chair. "Then you should have insisted Joe the doorman announce you. Sit. I'm feeling domestic—I'll make you some coffee."

Kate disappeared into the kitchen and Devlin stood awkwardly amidst Kate's stuff. There were flowers in three different vases, one on an oak dining-room table, one on an elaborately carved, fragile-looking table behind the blue-and-white sofa and another on the coffee table. Feeling big and awkward in this feminine room, Devlin decided to sit down on an overstuffed chair.

He settled back and, on the coffee table in front of him, saw the baby sweater Kate was knitting. He sat bolt upright and looked away from the little bundles of wool. He was a fool. A stupid, blithering idiot. What was he doing at Kate Ross's home on a Sunday morning?

She was a woman he knew next to nothing about—
her apartment and her fondness for knitting under-
lined that fact again. Hard-nosed, aggressive Kate Ross
lived amongst all this feminine fluff? But then, for what
he really knew of women maybe they all lived like this.

From the sounds of the fridge and cupboards being
opened and closed, Robert realized that Kate was pre-
paring a lot more than coffee.

He tugged at his tie. She was humming in the
kitchen. Was this what it was like to have a wife? Idiot,
he told himself and cleared his throat.

"Did you say something?" She peered out from between the swinging doors.

"No, nothing." Her hair was all loose and curly
around her face. His fingers itched to touch it, to run
his hands through it as he kissed her.

"I'll just be another minute," she promised.

Robert continued to sit uncomfortably. He didn't
know a damn thing about Kate. He didn't even like her
very much.

But that wasn't true. He liked her energy, her joy, her
determination. And he'd dreamed of her for the last
three nights. Of her and him. Together. Hot and sweaty
together. He tugged at his tie again. What did he think
he was accomplishing by coming to visit her? This
could have waited until tomorrow, but he'd seized the
chance to see her.

Idiot, he thought again. How could he be attracted to
her if he didn't understand her? He had no idea what
possessed her to want to be a mother. Without a husband. At the risk of her career.

She somehow believed she was strong enough to create a family alone.

Because of that, he wanted to help her. Which was why he was here. Which was also ridiculous because he didn't approve.

He noted how large and rough his hands appeared as he picked up the knitting needles, the pastel-colored skeins of wool tangling behind. Bunnies. There were little bunnies in blue and pink on the tiny sweater.

"I'm trying to cover the bases. The pink and the blue." Kate smiled wistfully at the sweater as she set down a large tray on the coffee table. Robert moved too slowly to help her. Along with a carafe of coffee and one mug were glasses of orange juice, cinnamon rolls and fresh strawberries. "Since I was so...scientific about the baby, I thought I shouldn't know the sex. At least I can do that part more traditionally."

For a second, as Kate stood with her arms crossed before him, Devlin thought she was going to confront him as she had the last time he'd arrived unannounced. But the mood this time was homier, almost comfortable. Kate was all softness in her curls, lace and bare feet. As if noticing his gaze, Kate belted her robe as she sat on the couch and poured him a mug of coffee. "You take it black, I remember." She picked up a glass of juice and settled back. "Can't enjoy coffee anymore. That's the worse part of having to get up at the crack of dawn."

"It's ten-thirty," Robert spluttered as she'd expected him to.

"On a Sunday, that *is* the crack of dawn." Kate

looked down as she swung her foot back and forth then raised mischievous eyes to his. She liked teasing Robert, she realized. It was nice having him in her home. If only she could keep him in the living room in her fantasies, and not let him into the bedroom. "I've never met anyone like you, Robert Devlin. Certainly no one who wears a jacket and tie on an unexpected Sunday-morning visit. I'm beginning to think you sleep in them."

He stiffened and remained silent.

"Don't mind me, Devlin," Kate said softly, taken aback by the suddenly bleak look on his face. Too often she hit the wrong note with him. She wished she understood him better. Well, she was going to try. He was her big secret—the father of her child. *Their daughter.* The thought frightened her a little, so she rushed on, "I'm a little silly in the morning. I didn't mean to offend you."

"It's about Gina," Devlin said without preamble.

"Good heavens, Devlin. I'm not going to say anything about the two of you." Kate's voice sounded a little too brittle for her liking.

Devlin flashed her a curious look and Kate wondered why she'd never noticed how masculine he was. Why she'd ever considered him unattractive. The expensive suits he wore covered a well-conditioned body, no padding or expert tailoring were needed. He had absolutely great shoulders: strong and wide. His face was all hard lines and angles, his eyes dark, his lips full and sensual. She could imagine those lips pressed against her skin, hot and exploring, covering every inch of her...

Goodness! Kate felt heat warm her entire body. She'd read that pregnant women experienced increased sexual desire, but this was insane. This was Devlin. He was involved with Gina King, Kate reminded herself, and she wasn't the kind of woman who set out to steal another woman's guy. Moreover, long ago she had vowed never to involve herself with anyone at work. Even more, she told herself, she and Devlin were competing for the same prize.

She knew that Anderson was setting them up. That he expected one of them to emerge the clear victor from this emergency situation. Most important, *she* wanted to save From Mother's Kitchen. The baby foods the Carlyle scientists had created were excellent, and available at a reasonable price. The development team had done a fabulous job creating natural, healthy, convenient products. From Mother's Kitchen conveyed a hominess and goodness that they wanted associated along with the convenience.

Somehow, Grannie had Carlyle's product and their campaign. It was so damn frustrating! Everyone had worked so hard on this project. They deserved to make it to the marketplace first, and succeed or fail on the strength of their product.

It really irked her that Goodspoon had cheated. Kate enjoyed competition, wasn't above trying to lead the opposition down the wrong path, but corporate espionage was beyond her. She wanted to succeed because she deserved it. Because whatever product she'd helped create was the best.

That was why she also respected Devlin. He was like her in that one regard.

Devlin began, "Gina did some investigating. She knows one of the admins at Goodspoon."

"And?" Could Gina have possibly learned where the leak came from? Kate knew that too many invisible fingers were pointed at her. It was the first time she'd found herself in such a vulnerable position. She was more used to being the rising star, the girl with the bright future. Before Carlyle, her career had been one success after another. After finishing college with a double major in business and English, she'd begun as a copywriter for a big Chicago ad agency. From account executive she'd moved to one of her accounts and become product manager. From chewing gum she'd moved to soups and then cosmetics. There she'd realized that environmental concerns were gaining a foothold in the market and her company had been among the first to create all-natural, not-tested-on-animals cosmetics, soaps and fragrances. That's when Carlyle Industries had wooed and won her corporate hand.

"Did Gina find out who, how..." Kate pressed a hand over her nervous stomach and was glad she was sitting down.

"Remember Rick Walker?"

Kate remembered the all-American preppie boy all too clearly. He'd been a junior account executive in Jennifer's public relations department when, after six months on the job, Jennifer began to hear a lot of quiet complaints about the man's wandering hands and expectations for closing a deal. "It took Jennifer six months to document the case against him before he could be fired for sexual harassment." Kate had been so busy with From Mother's Kitchen that she hadn't really known many details of the situation until Rick was gone.

"I know. We had a hard time convincing some of the women to talk, but eventually we had enough proof to get rid of him."

"We?"

"I worked quite closely with Jennifer." He looked at her, puzzled. "I thought you knew."

"Er, no...I was so involved with From Mother's Kitchen..." As usual she'd been so wrapped up in her own projects that she'd paid very little attention to Jennifer's concerns. She tried to quash her sudden ridiculous jealously that Jennifer and Devlin had worked closely together. Naturally Devlin liked Jennifer more than he liked her; they suited each other so much better. Jennifer was beautiful and talented and reasonable. She respected rules. She could make any man want her with just a smile. For the first time, Kate was glad that Jennifer had been cynical about romance for the past year.

"Well, anyway, we tried to exclude Walker from as much sensitive material as possible, but—"

"From Mother's Kitchen was entering the advertising stage," Kate realized. "Walker would have had access."

"Even more incriminating, Walker spent a lot of time in the production labs."

"You mean he stole the formulae? Just walked in and waltzed out with the recipes?"

"I'm sure it was a little more complicated than that, but basically...yes."

"But how can we be sure it was him? He may have been a pig but we don't know that he was a thief." Even with someone like Walker, Kate didn't like to find him guilty without sufficient proof.

"One of Gina's friends works in Accounting at Grannie Goodspoon. She said that they've cut several very large checks to Rick Walker. For consulting services. In six figures."

"Oh my." Kate was relieved and angry. "I can hardly believe he'd stoop so low."

"It seems our Mr. Walker didn't have a lot of ethics to begin with. I'll tell Anderson tomorrow what we've learned. Now we can concentrate on fixing the problem. We don't need to worry about Goodspoon knowing what we're up to."

"Devlin, thank you. I can't begin to say what this means."

"Maybe now you can stop worrying so much and get some sleep."

Surprised, Kate looked up at him and saw some undefinable emotion in his eyes. A little embarrassed at how protective he had become of her, she teased, "Why, Devlin, I swear under that gruff exterior lurks the heart of a hero." At the way he broke eye contact and stood, Kate knew she had said the wrong thing.

Jennifer would have known how to handle Devlin. Again, Kate quelled her unreasonable jealousy and, to stop him from leaving, took his hand.

He looked down at her much smaller hand—soft and graceful, the nails painted pale pink—and felt stupid and awkward once more. Another man could have answered Kate in the same light flirtatious style—told her she looked beautiful. He wanted to be able to do that, to tell her that he liked this room. That he wished he'd woken up in her bed with her and held the sweet red strawberries for her sweet red lips to taste.

All he could do was stand unmoving, terrified by the sight of their hands together, wanting so much more and unable to do a damn thing about it. If he wasn't careful, he'd pull her into his arms and ruin everything. No, he needed to proceed slowly. He needed time to consider why he was so inexplicably attracted to the infuriating, irresponsible, stubborn Kate Ross.

"I'm sorry, Devlin," Kate said. "Somehow I'm always saying the wrong thing when I want to tell you how much I appreciate everything you've done for me." Impulsively, she stood on tiptoe and kissed him on the cheek. "Thank you."

Devlin continued to stand awkwardly, unsure of what to do.

"And thank Gina, as well. I'll talk to her tomorrow, I really owe her one."

Finally they were back to ground he could navigate.

"We should invite Gina onto the baby-food team. She has a lot of good ideas we could use."

Kate felt the hurt clear down to her toes. So Devlin

had rushed over to tell her the news, not because he'd wanted to set her mind to rest, but to get Gina onto the team. She wondered if Gina knew how lucky she was to have a man like Devlin. Kate didn't have a choice, but she tried, "I realize she's been wanting to get on the management track for some time, and that she's competent, but do you really think it's a good idea?"

"She'll be a strong addition. And we owe her, Kate."

Kate nodded her agreement; she'd known Devlin would overrule her objections. And she did owe Gina. But the enjoyment of working with Devlin faded now that she would be working with Devlin and his lover.

7

WALKER WASN'T the only leak at Carlyle Industries. On Monday morning, Lipp called Kate and Robert into his office and swore them to secrecy.

"Someone logged onto my computer yesterday. I always keep the time log running for security." Lipp rubbed his temples and Kate thought she heard him groan, but that couldn't be possible. The production head was always in control.

"What records did the intruder get into?" She was almost afraid of the answer.

"All of the revised production dates and shipping."

"Oh my." Kate felt ill.

Robert slammed his fist on the coffee table. "Damn it." He stood up quickly, practically knocking over the chair, and began to pace. "I thought Walker was the source of our trouble. Now this. I can't believe someone we know is doing this to Carlyle. Someone we trust." Robert stayed frozen by the window with his back to her, but Kate could see his anger in the way he held his body.

"Walker was only here a short time," she said. "This isn't the first time that Grannie Goodspoon has known our plans." That little problem had occurred to Kate last night as she'd tossed and turned, trying not to imagine Robert and Gina together.

"At least Goodspoon didn't get access to our new marketing campaign," Lipp said.

At that, Robert turned to face Kate and smiled grimly. "It's not much of a campaign at the moment."

"It will be," Kate assured them both. "Inspiration hasn't struck yet, but soon...I'm sure."

"I hope inspiration knows there's a deadline," Robert said dryly and Kate prickled.

He just didn't understand how she worked. It would all come together. It always did. And it would again. She hoped. "How are we going to keep our campaign a secret? The traitor could be anyone." She didn't add, even one of us, but she thought it just for a second. What if Lipp wanted to throw everyone off his trail? What if it was Robert?

No, she was becoming paranoid. She needed to trust both of these men. As her mind began to tackle the problem facing Carlyle, she spoke her thoughts out loud. "I'll use a really small team on the initial creative campaign. Once we've established our hook, we can spread the information. By then it will be too late for good old Grannie to change her campaign."

"Excellent," Robert said. "I'll tell Gina."

"Gina!" Kate was shocked. Surely he couldn't be serious. It would be fine to have Gina on the team afterward, but not for the most important planning and development stage. "I was thinking of asking Jennifer and Steven from my department."

"I trust Gina completely," Robert said implacably.

"We can use her help. Unless you have some reason for not wanting her?"

He looked at her so blankly that Kate had the urge to smack him. Well, all right, so she didn't have any valid objections, but that sure didn't mean she had to like it. She shrugged, then nodded her head in agreement.

Robert turned to Lipp. "I suggest we keep this information between us for the time being. Whoever accessed your records had to have a company pass, keys and your code word. Let's all be extra careful from now on."

Robert followed Kate out of Lipp's office. "Damn but this is a mess."

"I have a hard time believing it myself." She noticed he was looking at her with concern, and wished he really meant it. But she'd seen him look at everyone on his staff in the same manner. "Well, if I want to get anything done before the eleven o'clock meeting, I'd better get to work," she added nervously. How did the man get her so hot and sweaty so quickly?

Robert reached out and touched her shoulder. "Are you all right, Kate? You look...different today."

"I'm fine," she lied and escaped down the hallway. Fine, if that meant staying up most of the night thinking about the father of her child. And the baby. And Carlyle. And Gina. And, well, just *everything!*

How had she ever let her life get so complicated?

Less than an hour later, Kate and Jennifer were walking along the same plush hallway toward the boardroom. Its quiet elegance soothed Kate's frazzled nerves.

"How long have Devlin and Gina been involved?" Kate asked.

"Devlin and Gina? I never heard a thing about it. Really?" At Kate's nod, Jennifer considered. "I'm usually much better connected to the grapevine, but Robert is a very private person. I think it's nice, him and Gina, they'd make a good couple."

That was not the answer she'd wanted to hear. "I thought Devlin didn't date," Kate grumbled.

"You want him to live like a corporate monk? I think Gina could be good for him, help him unwind. Or did you want him for yourself now that you know—"

"Don't even say it. I don't want to talk about it. Besides, Devlin levered me into inviting her onto the baby-food team."

"Gina is being underutilized as Benson's secretary." They had reached the boardroom. Jennifer's eyes widened as she studied Kate. "Oh my God, you're wearing a blue suit and white blouse. You look exactly like a senior executive. You're going to make the announcement today."

Kate nodded. "After the news about Rick Walker seems like the perfect time to strike."

Jennifer closed her eyes for a second and took a deep breath. "Well, this should be interesting," she said and threw open the boardroom doors.

"I THOUGHT THEY HAD ALL turned to stone," Kate admitted back in Jennifer's office. Retreat to Jennifer's couch had seemed a much better idea than to her office where anyone and everyone could have found her.

"I've never seen Silver at a loss [for words.] [I al-]
ways thought his name suited h[im.]
And Lipp actually snapped his penc[il,]
agreed, massaging her temples. Kate[...]
about her pregnancy had created almo[st as...]
the last hostile-takeover bid. Even Jennifer look[ed ruf-]
fled—and she had already known.

"Anderson just sat there. He didn't twitch a muscle." What did that mean? Kate wondered. Her announcement that she was pregnant and there would be
no wedding—had been greeted with such stunned
amazement that she had no idea what Anderson
would do.

She covered her growing belly with her hands, cradling her baby. No matter what anyone else thought—
including Devlin—she was doing the right thing. She
wouldn't regret her actions even if Anderson fired her.
The idea frightened her and she shivered. Then she felt
the baby kick.

"Oh!" She smiled. Her daughter was reminding her
of what was important.

Jennifer looked at Kate curiously.

"It's the baby," she clarified. "She's kicking."

"What's it like?" Jennifer asked. She moved toward
Kate. "Can I...?"

"Of course, here." She held Jennifer's hand over her
stomach. Her daughter did a little somersault and Kate
saw some unexpressed emotion cross Jennifer's face.

"That's incredible," Jennifer said softly. "You really
are going to be a mother."

Kate couldn't help giggling with joy and Jennifer joined in.

"I admire you, Kate," Jennifer said, hugging her friend. "I don't think I've told you that, but I do. You haven't let anyone or anything stop you from doing what you want. I hope I can learn to be more like you."

Kate looked at her best friend in surprise. "But I always wish to be more like you," she exclaimed.

Jennifer shook her head. "Don't. I'm hiding. I'm not willing to take chances. Be who you are, Kate." She squeezed her hand. "You'll be just fine."

Kate wished she knew how to comfort Jennifer, but it was Jennifer who was going to have to change her own life.

And she had finally told everyone the truth about herself. She'd thrown the dice; let them lie where they may.

Now all she had to do was worry about the baby-food campaign. Of course, even that would no longer be a concern if after her announcement she no longer had a job.

"BUT HOW CAN YOU be pregnant, dear?" Kate's mother asked, her gentle eyes crinkling as she frowned. "You're not dating anyone."

"I went to a clinic, Mother. I was artificially inseminated." Kate was glad she had waited until dessert to break the news. Her brothers and sister and their spouses were staring at her blankly as if she had just announced that aliens had landed on Earth.

"You're having a test-tube baby?" her father demanded.

"Not exactly. Sort of." Artificial insemination clinics weren't how her parents expected to have grandchildren. She'd expected her parents to be shocked, but she'd also expected her brothers and sister to provide support. They could jump in at any point now, she thought with chagrin. As the silence stretched on, Kate decided to continue her story. "The point is, this is something I've given a lot of thought to. Especially after Todd ended the engagement."

"Maybe Todd will come back," her mother suggested. "I always liked him so much." Aline Ross's dearest goal in life was to have all her children happily married. Kate supposed that her confidence in her parenting abilities came from her own mother's example. Aline had devoted her life to her family and had been very happy.

Even now that her children were spread throughout the country, Aline was still in close touch with each of them. Greg, the lawyer, lived in Sarasota, Florida, and Tommy in New York. Tommy was the artistic, rebellious member of the family; they expected *him* to do the unconventional, not Kate. Kate had known that her mother would have a hard time understanding her decision. That's why she had come home to celebrate her mother's birthday and announce the news in person.

Kate sighed. This was even more complicated than she'd imagined. She wished that Anne and her husband had been able to make their mother's birthday dinner, but their youngest had come down with the chicken pox. "Todd is engaged to someone else, Mother."

"That bum!"

"No, Todd was right. I didn't want to marry him nearly as much as I want this baby. You all said I'd be a great mother." She turned to Greg and his wife, Janet. Tommy winked at her, but he'd have little sway over the family. Her father couldn't understand how Tommy could live in a loft—"a home without walls," he called it.

Janet answered. "Of course you will, Kate. We're just...surprised."

"Babies need two parents," Greg, the ever-practical, oldest son said.

"Now, honey, Kate is a very capable woman. I'm sure she'll manage," Janet insisted.

Kate smiled gratefully at her sister-in-law. Her brother was very traditional. Why hadn't she remembered all the arguments about Janet going back to work after the birth of their son? Greg had wanted Janet to stay home, just as his mother had done. Janet, however, had stood firm and returned to practise law. But she only worked part-time, Kate remembered.

"I have it all arranged," Kate said desperately. "A live-in nanny and an alternate baby-sitter."

"Nannies!" Greg snorted. "A child needs a full-time mother and a father."

"Now, Greg, don't go on so. Kate can do as she thinks is right. Times are different now," their mother soothed and reached over to pat Kate's hand.

Kate blinked away her tears.

"Of course we'll help, too," her mother added gamely. But Kate sensed her mother's doubt. Her parents were busy leading their own lives.

"We need a return to strong families." Greg had begun to sound more and more like Devlin than Kate cared to hear. These days she always knew what Devlin thought of any situation—she could hear his voice in her head. Go away, she told him. She was having enough trouble with her family, without Devlin.

In fact, Devlin could just stay out of her thoughts altogether. Then maybe she'd stop fantasizing about Devlin and she and baby making three.

AFTER AN ANXIETY-RIDDEN week, Kate still hadn't heard anything from Anderson and she'd had no inspiration for the From Mother's Kitchen campaign and no one had been uncovered as the corporate spy and Devlin had barely spoken to her and she'd gained seven pounds and couldn't fit into any of her work clothes. So she called her sister, cried and then they went shopping.

Anne lived in a suburb of Chicago only an hour's drive away. The sisters were able to get together a couple of times a month. Usually, Kate drove to Anne's ranch-style home and enjoyed a family dinner. Anne's natural ability as a mother had also confirmed Kate's desire to be a mom, as well. She imagined her daughter playing with Anne's children.

"They expect women to wear this?" Kate demanded as she held a flowered and frilled dress against herself in the store's mirror. She'd hoped that the suburban mall would have good maternity dresses.

"I wish I could loan you some of my maternity clothes, but since I was working out of home, I wore a lot of leggings and sweaters." Anne's job as a freelance journalist had allowed her a lot of flexibility.

"And then you stayed home with the baby. Do you think what I'm doing is wrong, Anne?" That idea had begun to enter her head too often for her liking.

"Oh, no, Kate. We all do it our own way. I was lucky that I had a career where I could take some time out without being penalized. Here, try this." Anne handed her a tailored blouse with wide sleeves. "By the way, I understand dinner at the folks' wasn't exactly a success."

"That's an understatement. Dad never said a word after I made my announcement. Mom recovered eventually, but I could tell she didn't agree with what I was doing. And Greg was just impossible!"

"I know. Janet phoned." Anne found a pair of navy slacks and passed them over. "Greg seems to become more and more conservative. He and Janet are trying to have a second child."

"Really? I thought that Janet wanted to move up in her law firm." Was it really impossible to keep up with your career? Kate worried.

Anne grinned. "Our dear brother is going to stay home with the baby for a year. That's their agreement."

"Greg?" Kate couldn't believe it.

"Janet knows our brother a lot better than we do. I think he might make a good stay-at-home dad."

Kate giggled, but then she stopped. What about her? She still hoped to be a successful career woman—she wanted that vice presidency. She also knew herself. After she achieved *that* goal, what *else* would she want?

Sighing, she held up a polka-dot monstrosity. Was she wrong, Kate wondered miserably, to think she could have it all?

"NOT ONLY DID HE GET Ms. Ross pregnant and then dump her, but he's engaged to another woman." Kate stopped dead still, just before turning the corner to the coffee machine. She forced herself forward and in a very calm voice said, "Mr. Miller is not the father of my baby. The only part of the rumor that's true is that he is very happily engaged to another woman and I am glad for him." She turned a steely gaze on Cynthia from Accounting and Bill from PR. "Are there any more questions I can answer for you?" she asked in her best schoolmarm voice.

"No, Ms. Ross." Cynthia bolted, leaving her coffee cup behind.

Bill only gulped and nodded and then fled. At least he took his mug with him. She took juice out of the fridge and assured herself that next week Carlyle Industries would have some new scandal to discuss.

At least she hoped so. She took a sip of the juice, turned around to leave and bumped into Robert.

"Careful." His strong arms held her by the shoulders. He studied her with concern. Kate felt tears threaten and she looked away quickly. Robert was only being kind. He was kind to everyone.

"I couldn't help overhearing," he said. "Don't let the talk trouble you. There will be a new topic for the watercooler next week."

Kate smiled weakly. "I hope so." She backed away from him. "I have some reports I have to finish." Hurrying back to her office, she berated herself for being a fool. How she would have loved to have leaned her head against his strong shoulders and have him hold her.

But Robert Devlin was involved with someone else. No matter what her overactive imagination and hormones were fantasizing, she needed to keep that in mind. Robert Devlin was not for her.

"KATE, I've given your situation a great deal of thought," Anderson said.

Kate rubbed her sweaty palms against her skirt. It had been two weeks since she'd revealed her pregnancy and she'd been waiting for Anderson to call her into his office. Now she wondered why she'd been so eager to get this over with.

"It's not the way we did things in my day—the man would have had to marry you, not abandon you!—but still, I realize that times are different. And that single mothers will also invest in our new baby-food line. Hell, your new area of expertise may give you an unfair advantage over the male executives." Anderson laughed over his joke, but Kate realized he meant it. He thought she might be a benefit to Carlyle. As he examined her growing middle, Kate felt like a prime beef cow being assessed for the value of its steaks.

"So, I still consider you a viable candidate for the vice-president job. Naturally I expect you to take off a couple of weeks after the birth of the baby, but you should be able to continue doing some work from home. You've always been a hard worker—I'm sure you'll manage just fine." He gave her a nod. "I'll let the other candidates know they should still consider you competition."

"WHAT ARE YOU EATING?" Jennifer demanded.

"This?" Kate asked guiltily. "It's just ice cream."

"With chocolate sauce, cherries, chocolate peanut-butter bits..." Jennifer frowned as she examined the dish more closely. "Caramel sauce, whipped cream and...olives?"

"I had this craving," Kate admitted.

"But did you have to put them all together? Next time warn me when you're going to eat something like this." Jennifer shuddered dramatically. "I wanted to remind you that I've scheduled the advertising-promotion meeting for Friday morning."

Kate ate three spoonfuls of her concoction. It was really good; she wondered why she'd never thought of it before her pregnancy. "I haven't forgotten. But I'm dreading it. Our original campaign is being copied by Grannie Goodspoon and they have an advantage over us because of the grandmother image."

"Grannie will slaughter our fresh-faced mom," Jennifer agreed.

"We need something else, but what?" Kate scooped another spoonful of the ice cream feeling happy—and worried. Until her pregnancy, she'd never known it was possible to feel so many conflicting emotions at once. Joy and pride over her baby. Worry over how she would handle it all. Concern over the baby-food line, the promotion, her career.

But the cause of most of her jumbled emotions was, of course, Robert Devlin.

"Ms. Ross."

Kate raised her tired eyes from Lipp's production schedule to her doorway where a timid-looking Gina King stood. She probably felt uncomfortable because Kate knew about her and Devlin. "Come in, Gina," she said softly. There was no reason to take her jealousy—she'd finally admitted to herself what she'd been feeling—out on Gina.

"I just wanted to thank you for including me on the baby-food team."

"You deserved it, especially after what you learned about Rick Walker."

"Still, it was very generous. This is the opportunity I've been looking for."

"I guess Benson wasn't too happy with the news," Kate guessed. He'd try to make Gina's life hell, Kate suddenly realized. She should have thought of that. Gina remained silent—no complaints about her boss. Still, Kate knew how petty Benson could be. He'd probably double Gina's workload, and when you added that onto the workload of the task force and her family life...

"Maybe I could ask my assistant if she could provide you with some help over the next few weeks," Kate offered.

"Mr. Devlin has already done that with his assistant."

"Then if Mrs. Conte agrees, you'll have twice the help." How the devil did Devlin always think of these things before her? It wasn't just because he was involved with Gina, she knew. He paid attention and fixed problems for everyone. Herself included.

"Thank you, Ms. Ross. There's one other thing." Gina hesitated.

"Go on," Kate urged.

Gina took a deep breath and met Kate's gaze straight on. "It's after the baby's born...I know you have a nanny, but, well, with kids, especially babies, it can be overwhelming at times. So, if you need help or someone to talk to, I'd be happy to do what I can."

At the woman's earnest and caring expression, Kate realized she should listen. Gina had two kids and had been raising them by herself for a long time.

"Maybe you should sit down and tell me about it," Kate suggested, pointing to her couch and leaving her desk. "I have a feeling you know a lot more about this than I can ever imagine."

"The kids, they're great," Gina began as she sat down, her natural openness returning. "But when you're doing it by yourself, taking courses, trying to get somewhere with your career, plus worrying about day care, there are days you come home when you'd give anything to have a partner." She smiled wearily and continued. "I know I should be concerned about nutrition, but when the kids are screaming in the back seat of the car for McDonald's, sometimes it's just easier to give in."

As Gina continued describing what it would be like to be a single mother, Kate listened intently and asked several questions.

Gina's own worries and concerns reflected Kate's. Kate already loved her baby more than she could have ever dreamed, but she also knew that she was facing uncharted territory.

And that was when her new marketing campaign was conceived.

8

"BOARDROOM BABY. That's the situation for women of the nineties—and the name of our new baby-food campaign." Kate pointed animatedly to the display boards she had managed to put together in a day.

Devlin leaned back and watched Kate in action. This is what she did best. Somehow, she intuitively hit upon the right idea for the campaign, and then she'd get the market research to back up her idea. Normally, this method infuriated him, but as Carlyle was running out of time, he was glad Kate's genius had struck. She'd left an urgent message that he needed to attend an emergency meeting this evening. Since he rarely had social plans, it hadn't been a problem. Since he had no desire for any woman other than Kate, he'd been living the life of a monk.

"Forget all this From Mother's Kitchen crap—working women don't need any more guilt laid on them, subconsciously or not," Kate said. "The average mother today is performing a balancing act of titanic proportions between career, children and housework." Kate read from statistics. "The average working woman spends more than thirty hours a week on household chores compared to ten for men. That's a full-time job on top of a full-time job.

"Women want baby food that is nutritious, whole-some, affordable and convenient. Once we have a foot-hold in the baby-food market we'll be able to expand into children's food. Gina pointed out that she's look-ing for exactly those products for her kids.

"So we don't pretend with these women. We admit to the reality of their lives and that our baby food comes from a company that understands and wants to help."

Kate looked up from her paperwork and continued enthusiastically, waving her arms. "We use real testi-monials from women and from the scientists who cre-ated Carlyle baby foods. And then—it'll be easier if I show you." Kate put a video into the VCR. "This is rough but it will give you an idea of what the advertis-ing could be like."

Devlin had seen Kate, Gina and Jennifer racing around the building throughout yesterday—and as he now watched their work on the video, he realized that what they had managed to create was brilliant. They had testimonials from a number of female employees discussing the never-ending list of tasks involved with child rearing and managing careers. The camera then cut to Carlyle scientists, male and female, talking about their goals: nutrition, no artificial additives, conve-nience. Added to this was the montage of one woman rushing through her day—breakfast, feed the baby, day care, work, pick up the kids, dinner. At the end of the segment, after using Carlyle products, the woman finally has some time to herself, a candlelight bubble bath, and then the viewer sees her clad in a sexy negligée approaching her appreciative husband with Whitney Houston's "I'm Your Baby Tonight" swelling on the sound track.

At the end of the video the three women turned to Devlin, waiting. "It's fantastic," he said and meant every word. "A completely different approach from Grannie Goodspoon's. More honest. Let's run it by Anderson ASAP and then get the agency on the campaign. Congratulations, Kate."

Kate beamed at him and he felt good all over. He'd been trying to stay away from her, but it was impossible. Even the background checks on the employees couldn't keep his mind off Kate. He wished he could tell her about the investigator he'd hired, but the less people who knew about it the better.

Kate continued to smile at him. "Thank Gina. She's the one who gave me the idea."

Gina blushed. "Ms. Ross, Kate, is being too generous. She listened to me talk and created this. She's amazing." Gina was clearly awestruck.

"This calls for a celebration," Jennifer said. "I'll call the Chinese place."

While Jennifer went to order the food, Devlin and Kate compared notes. He had a few suggestions. "My only complaint is that the husband was completely irrelevant except as a lover."

"That's certainly not irrelevant."

Devlin let her teasing wash over him. "What I mean is that you've completely ignored the role of the father. Men today are involved."

"All the women I talked to barely mentioned their

husbands, if they had one." She nodded toward Gina, who was packing up the display.

"They may have also been influenced by who was asking the questions—a woman who's going to be a single mother," Devlin insisted rationally.

"Devlin, you are so old-fashioned. I wonder what your upbringing was like..." Kate let the words trail off, and he felt uncomfortable under her scrutiny. "But you're right. We don't want to offend our male market share. I'll have the agency include some fathers. Happy daddies bouncing healthy laughing babies." She leaned closer and he smelled her flowery scent. Since she'd become pregnant, she'd chosen prettier clothes, a lighter scent than the spicy fragrance she'd worn before. "Would you like to bounce a giggly baby on your knee," she queried, looking at him with a teasing smile, moving even closer so that their faces were only inches apart. "Or would you prefer a woman?" Her gaze fell to his lips and he had the wild urge to pull her into his lap and kiss her until her laughter was replaced by desire.

The same desire that had been haunting him for days. He had no idea when it had happened, but he wanted Kate Ross. He found her growing figure unbearably erotic—his dreams were full of her, lush and womanly, dressed in that Victorian robe as he held her, touched her, kissed her.

For a suspended moment, as Kate leaned toward him, her moist lips parted, he thought she was going to kiss him. Then Jennifer breezed into the room carrying sacks of take-out food. "Someone, help," she called and, the spell broken, Kate moved to take a bag from Jennifer.

Gina, who'd returned from putting away the display, poured the wine for herself, Jennifer and Devlin and offered Kate a glass of apple juice. Then while she, Jennifer and Devlin were still trying to find the cutlery, Gina had the boardroom table set up with the food, pulled the cutlery out of the drawer they hadn't looked into and found two candles and lit them. Kate was only grateful that they were eating Chinese so that the super-efficient Gina couldn't cut her meat for her. Heavens, when had she become such a shrew? she wondered. Since when had Gina become such a threat?

The answer was unfortunately too easy for her conscience to answer: ever since she'd learned that Gina and Devlin were an item.

Still, she scolded herself, that did not give her reason to find fault with a woman who was capable of doing everything. Why, Gina personified the woman Boardroom Baby wanted to reach. If they needed a spokesperson, there wasn't anyone better. That stopped Kate again. She had to admit that she'd considered herself the role model for the new campaign. But the reality was that Gina knew much more than she did. And, Kate had financial advantages that Gina was struggling to achieve.

Gina raised her wineglass, her face animated. "Here's to the success of Boardroom Baby," she toasted.

"To truth in advertising," Jennifer added with a wicked grin.

Devlin toasted silently, watching Gina's happy expression. He cared for the woman a great deal, Kate realized. And why wouldn't he? Gina was attractive and smart. Fun to be around. She had a great figure and was probably fabulous in bed.

Kate automatically ate some of the food but didn't taste any. She wondered if Robert spent the weekends with Gina and her children, if he'd become a replacement father for Gina's kids.

Robert Devlin is the father of my baby, she found herself wanting to shout.

She put her plate on the mahogany table, appalled at herself. She had no rights in this situation.

"Is something wrong, Kate?" Gina asked her, concern written all over her face.

Plus, Gina was nice, Kate added to her mental list of what made the woman annoyingly perfect. "No, nothing's wrong. I'm just a little tired. Maybe I'll go home." She sounded exhausted and depressed even to herself.

"I could drive you," Jennifer said.

"Thanks, but you're at the opposite end of town. I'll leave my car here and take a cab." Smiling weakly at the celebrants, Kate made her escape to her office. Once there, she didn't know what to do. Before she had learned Robert Devlin was the father of her baby, she had always known what to do.

For the first time in a long time she felt weak. She leaned her forehead against the cool glass of her floor-to-ceiling window and closed her eyes, savoring the cold, letting it counter her fevered forehead. She didn't know how long she stood there until she felt a hand on her shoulder and turned in surprise.

It was Devlin. "Kate. Are you all right? I didn't mean to startle you, but you didn't hear me when I called your name."

She was ridiculously glad to see him. To know that he had followed her because he was worried about her. That wasn't any more than he would do for any employee of Carlyle, a little voice reminded her. Still, she was happy and had to stop herself from leaning against him and burying herself in his arms.

"Kate?"

He wasn't wearing his glasses and Kate lost herself in the dark brown of his eyes. They had depths and mysteries she'd never been aware of until recently. His rugged face was all strength and perfect lines. "Kate?" he asked again and touched her face.

He felt it, too—she could see by the way his eyes widened and a muscle at the side of his mouth moved. It was like an electric charge from Devlin to herself— and yet more. It was as if she'd always been waiting for his touch. The feel of his skin, so different from hers, thrilled her as his strong but gentle fingers stroked her cheek.

She gasped as his hand cupped her chin and his thumb stroked her bottom lip. Every nerve in her body was sensitized by that one action, humming, alive. Her gaze was on his lips as his thumb stroked her bottom lip again. Her lips parted and so did his, as if in response.

"Oh." The sound was low and sensual and came

from her. Kate met Devlin's gaze and was shocked by the need she saw in his eyes. It was as if they were the only two people in the world. Man and woman.

"Kate," he said, and that was all the encouragement she needed to step closer to him. She didn't have to do anything else as his arms wrapped around her and he lowered his head to kiss her. Mesmerized, she watched as his eyes came closer, dark, full of questions and wanting. Then his lips were on hers and she had to close her eyes.

She'd never felt anything like it before. She hadn't known she could lose herself so completely in a kiss. She lost all sense of who she was, except a woman overcome, consumed by desire.

His lips were hard and soft, powerful and gentle. He nibbled from one corner of her mouth to the other and then pressed his lips full against hers, as if he hadn't had her attention before. He took and gave, and need spiraled within her.

With his tongue he demanded entrance to her mouth and she eagerly opened, meeting his conquering strokes with teasing ones of her own that slowed the pace. They each learned about the other.

She dragged her hands through his dark hair, reveling in the luxury of touching him. He let out a moan when she ran her fingertips over his ear, so she did it again.

Devlin tore his lips from hers for a breath of air, but before she could complain he sucked her lower lip into his mouth, and she melted. If his arms hadn't been holding her upright, she would have collapsed onto the floor.

As if sensing her incredible need, Devlin pulled her even closer, so that she could feel every strong masculine inch of him. His hands moved from her back to her hips and he held her tight against him as he pushed his arousal against the juncture of her thighs.

At the simulated lovemaking, she felt herself grow wet. She wanted him inside of her. Deep and pulsing. She threw back her head, exposing her throat to him and sighed.

So quickly that she didn't know how it happened, Kate was standing by herself. Reflexively, she caught herself from falling by grabbing a corner of her desk. Devlin stood three feet away, straightening his tie. Clearly the kiss hadn't affected him the way it had her. She looked away from him, embarrassed. She would have been willing to fall onto the floor with him, roll around on the carpet and...

Devlin was the one who had stopped. He had come here to see if she was all right. What had she done but thrown herself at him!

She hung her head and wished she could blame it on her pregnancy, but she wouldn't lie to herself. She wanted Devlin and if he hadn't stopped then, they'd be having sex right now. At the mental image of them naked on the floor, Kate raised her eyes to him.

"Kate, I'm sorry," Devlin began. "It was inexcusable of me to take advantage of you in your situation—"

"You didn't take advantage," Kate said quietly, but Devlin seemed to ignore her.

"It won't happen again," he insisted.

Kate pulled herself together. It felt like a slap in the face. Devlin couldn't have made it clearer that he wasn't interested. That the kiss had been an aberration. She threw back her shoulders and calmly walked toward the coat hook and picked up her coat. Luckily, Devlin didn't help her put it on. She wasn't sure what she would have done if he'd touched her. She had her pride.

"We'll pretend this never happened," she said in a remarkably composed, firm voice. Then she nodded and left her office with him still standing in it.

If only she could leave the memory of their kiss as easily.

Two LONG WEEKS LATER, Devlin still couldn't get Kate Ross out of his mind. Or what it had been like to kiss her.

Last night when he'd been eating dinner with the Blackwoods, he'd found himself talking about Kate. Alan had looked at Robert with open surprise and accused him of being smitten with her.

He tried to rationalize to himself that his attraction was only natural since he and Kate were working so closely together, but he knew that wasn't the truth. The truth was, lately, not much of their work overlapped. Each facet of Boardroom Baby was running smoothly. The advertising campaign was almost finished, and Lipp had managed to speed up production. Boardroom Baby and From Grannie's Kitchen would be vying for supermarket supremacy in a few weeks.

Whoever had been selling information to Goodspoon was laying low—although there was nothing that could hurt the Boardroom Baby campaign now, he hoped. So far, the private investigator he'd hired had learned nothing.

No, what he felt for Kate Ross was quite different—and absolutely ridiculous. On the occasions when they'd had to go over reports together in her office, he'd been tempted to drag her into his arms and make mad, passionate love to her—on the carpet, if necessary—until she forgot everything except him.

It wasn't only her sexy lips and soft skin that beckoned him. He liked the way she argued with him, stuck out her chin and tried to figure out how to manipulate him into doing things her way.

He wanted to touch her growing stomach and feel the baby. And that was exactly what was wrong with him. Even if he agreed with Kate's decision to have a child as a single parent—and he didn't—he wasn't the kind of man to be a father. And that was what Kate needed in her life at this moment. A man who'd be willing to be a lover to her and a father to her baby. A man who would stay around.

He, however, had absolutely no track record when it came to commitment. He was terrible at anything to do with families. He didn't *know* anything about families. All of his experiences in life had taught him that he was meant to remain alone. The lonely boy who had learned to fend for himself was grown-up, but he wasn't any different. He'd never fallen in love. He'd dated, but no woman had ever fallen in love with him.

Clearly, he was one of those people who weren't capable of love.

He could never be a father to Kate Ross's baby.

Telling himself that he had to keep his hands off the woman, to keep his fantasies hidden, Devlin began to cross out Kate's overinflated promotion numbers when he heard her hurrying down the hallway toward his office. For weeks now he'd been able to recognize the sound of Kate's footsteps.

She burst into his office. "Robert, it's the print advertising." She threw a pile of magazine advertisements onto his desk. "They're wonderful. I wanted you to see them right away. If we approve these today, our ads could begin a whole week before Grannie's." Kate smiled wickedly. "I have friends at Grannie's ad agency. They don't even have color irises of their ads."

Kate was wearing a loose ivory-colored top over a short red skirt and red shoes. Tearing his eyes away from her great legs, he studied the ads, full-color montages of the typical working-woman's day. "These are good." He initialed the corner and handed them back to her and returned to the file he'd been working on. He didn't want to encourage Kate to stay.

"Oh."

At the sound, Robert couldn't help looking back at her. "Is something wrong? The baby?"

Kate shrugged. "Oh, no. The baby is wonderful. It's just, well..." Incredibly, Kate looked nervous. "This is the first part of the campaign we've managed to pull off before Grannie Goodspoon and I thought maybe we should celebrate."

"Celebrate?" Devlin managed to keep his voice calm even as his pulse began to race. She was making a *business* proposition, nothing more. Ever since the kiss, she had kept herself away from him. Which was the smart thing to do, he knew.

"Dinner," Kate said determinedly. "I want to invite you out to dinner."

It was only dinner, he told himself as he nodded his agreement. But somehow he and Kate always seemed to get themselves involved in so much more, despite their best intentions.

Dinner. It was only going to be dinner, he vowed.

9

ONCE AGAIN Robert Devlin found himself nodding to Joe the doorman and entering Kate's condominium. But this time, for the first time, he'd been invited. That made him incredibly nervous.

Kate met him at the door with a smile and hung up his coat. She wore a frilly apron. When she caught him staring, she laughed. "Don't let this fool you—I haven't suddenly turned into June Cleaver. I ordered in our dinner. This is just to keep my clothes clean as I dish out. The bar's over there." She pointed to the large bay window overlooking the ravine and headed back toward the kitchen.

Normally, Devlin didn't drink but he needed one tonight. As he poured himself a scotch he looked out at the park, at the kids playing Frisbee.

He should have said no. He should never have come to Kate Ross's home.

Why? part of him taunted. Did he really think Kate meant anything by the invitation other than a celebration for the job so far? Or possibly was it a chance for her to gauge her competition some more?

She hadn't invited him because she wanted them to be friends, because she had any...feelings for him. Devlin gulped down the drink and poured himself another. He was such a fool. Hadn't all the times he'd wanted someone to care for him—with no result—taught him anything?

"Robert!" Kate called from the kitchen.

Slamming his drink onto the bar, Robert raced to her. What if something was wrong? He found Kate leaning against the kitchen counter, her hands cupped over her belly. "What is it?" he demanded, for once not hiding his concern.

Kate took his hand. "It's the baby. She's having an aerobics workout. Feel." She placed his hand over her stomach and immediately he felt the movement.

"That's incredible."

Kate smiled her glorious smile at him and moved his hand a little lower. "And here, this seems to be a favorite area. I hope I'm not embarrassing you, but I don't often have anyone around when the baby is so active...and well, I just thought it would be nice to share it with you." Kate blushed.

"No, er, thank you," Devlin said, suddenly feeling uncomfortable touching Kate so intimately—especially after all the lascivious fantasies he'd been having about her. But he couldn't move his hand quite yet. He'd felt too uncomfortable to ask Betty Blackwood to let him touch her like this, as if he would be an intruder. But with Kate it felt okay.

Finally he dropped his hand and said thank you. Kate looked at him and shook her head. "You are an odd one, Devlin. There are times when I don't understand you at all."

He turned away. "There's not much to understand. I go to work and do a good job. End of story."

"There's a lot more to you than that." Kate picked up the take-out cartons she'd removed from the oven and began to carry them into the dining room. Devlin grabbed the plates and followed. "First, you know everything there is to know about Carlyle Industries and everyone working there," she said. "And you help everyone—including myself, who is supposed to be your archenemy."

"You were never my enemy."

"Rival, then. We want the same job, Devlin, and all you've done is support me." Kate busied herself opening the cartons, not looking at him. It made it easier to talk and she wanted to tell him what she thought.

"When you concluded I was a seduced and abandoned woman, you dragged the man you assumed had done me wrong over to my house so that he could have the chance to do the right thing and marry me.

"Then you learned that I'd gotten myself pregnant intentionally, and despite your obvious feelings that what I'm doing is wrong, all you've done is help me.

"How come some woman hasn't wrapped a wedding ring around your finger by now?" There, she'd finally asked the question she'd really wanted the answer to ever since she'd learned Devlin was the father of her baby. Ever since she'd been forced to look at him with new eyes and wondered...

At Robert's silence, Kate glanced at him. He was looking at her intently and she looked away quickly, embarrassed, and then returned her gaze to him. His eyes were dark and compelling. She wished she knew what he was thinking. How he felt about her. How he felt about Gina.

"I'm married to my job," he answered in a very calm voice. If he hadn't fidgeted with his glasses, Kate would have believed him. Damn, she thought, it had to be Gina.

Well, Gina might have been quicker off the mark than Kate, but that didn't mean she'd won the race, Kate decided. And she was beginning to realize that Devlin was a prize definitely worth winning.

"You haven't met the right woman," she said flirtatiously. "Or maybe you have and you just haven't noticed her."

That caught his attention. Devlin concentrated on her and Kate was frozen to her chair. As if a rubber band had suddenly been pulled tight, she felt the sexual tension zing between them. *Oh, please, God, let him feel it, too.* The neutral expression he wore—the one he assumed whenever a meeting became emotionally charged—told her he did. She breathed a sigh of relief. Immediately his eyes fell to her parted lips and Kate knew she'd throw herself into his arms if he made any kind of move toward her.

Robert held himself still, not trusting himself to move. If he did, he'd be all over Kate. She's a pregnant woman, he reminded himself. A vulnerable pregnant woman who needed his help. A trusting vulnerable pregnant woman who needed his help.

She was the sexiest woman he'd ever met.

What was wrong with him? Other men dreamed of

Playboy centerfolds, while he fantasized about a pregnant woman.

A gorgeous, increasingly voluptuous woman, the devil in him argued.

At work every day he had to fight to keep his hands to himself. And now, here in her home where she felt safe, all he could think about was dragging her off to the bedroom and making love to her until neither of them ever wanted anyone else again.

He took a step toward her and Kate rose out of her chair. He stopped. He couldn't do this. He stepped closer and stopped. He definitely shouldn't do this.

He moved to her, touched her shoulders and ran his hands along her arms, pulling her against him. Maybe Kate did need him. He would look after her.

"Oh, Robert," she said tremulously and smiled at him. He bent his head to her and her smile grew warmer. He felt need and joy hit him simultaneously as his lips touched hers.

Woman. She tasted female and he couldn't stop himself from tasting her more deeply, from tightening his arms around her so that her sexy curves fit against his body. Soft female flesh against solid male torso. Kate moaned and he deepened the kiss.

He wanted to conquer her. To show her how much he wanted her. How good he could make her feel.

Tell her that she was his woman.

He couldn't say the words but he could show her. Moving his head slightly so he could kiss her from a different angle, Robert let his hands begin to explore Kate's changing body. She was so soft, her hips and her breasts made to pleasure a man. She felt so good that he had a hard time remembering not to throw her on the ground and himself on top of her. Still, she must have sensed his desperate urgency because Kate suddenly broke out of his embrace.

She gasped and clutched her stomach.

"What is it?" he demanded, furious at himself. If he'd hurt her...

Kate straightened her bent shoulders and looked puzzled. "Oh, I think it was just a false contraction." She smiled weakly, but he could tell that she was worried. "I'm sure it's nothing." She took a step forward and then doubled over again. "No, no," she moaned, clutching her stomach again.

He caught her in his arms as she fell against him. Nothing serious could be wrong, he assured himself. He wouldn't let it be. Carrying her to the couch, he asked, "Kate, Kate, what's wrong?"

Her face glistened with sweat as she twisted on the couch trying to get comfortable. "Something's not right. The baby. Oh, God." She began to cry. "Something's wrong with the baby."

No, this couldn't be happening. Robert felt fear clutch his stomach but he knew he had to stay calm for Kate. He wrapped her in his arms and she clung to him. "Don't cry," he whispered into her hair. "I'm not going to let anything happen to you or your baby."

"It's too early for anything to happen to the baby!" Kate wailed.

Robert extricated himself and pulled her to her feet, then swept her into his arms.

"What are you doing?" she gasped and then cried as another pain hit her.

"I'm taking you to the hospital." He grabbed his keys and Kate's keys from the hallway table and walked as quickly as he could out of the apartment to the elevator. He murmured reassuring words to her as he silently cursed the elevator's slow arrival. Joe looked surprised as Robert strode out the door with Kate in his arms.

Opening the door of his black sports car, he helped Kate in. She gave him a trembling smile as he moved to the driver's side. "Did I ever tell you how surprised I was to learn that this car was yours?" Clearly, she was seeking a distraction from her worries.

He checked all of his mirrors, pulled out of the parking lot and began to expertly weave in and out of traffic. "You didn't expect conservative old Devlin to have a flashy car," he soon replied, humoring her.

"Exactly." Kate gasped again. She looked so pale and afraid, Devlin tried to keep the conversation going.

"What do you think now?"

"I'm glad you have it. Can you go any faster?"

Devlin accelerated. Nothing, absolutely nothing was going to happen to Kate.

She'd closed her eyes and was biting her lip so hard he could see blood.

"I've never asked anyone to marry me because I've always been afraid," he said, harking back to their earlier conversation.

Kate's eyes popped open and she stared at him with curiosity. "You're not afraid of anything," she accused.

Devlin changed lanes, shot past a BMW and glanced at Kate. He had her undivided attention.

"I spent my childhood in foster homes. My mother abandoned me. I was also a fat, truculent child who wore glasses as thick as cola-bottle bottoms. When the other kids were adopted I got angry. The angrier I got the more unappealing I became, even to my foster parents. I changed homes twelve times between the ages of seven and eighteen."

"How sad," Kate said quietly.

"I learned that brains were my way out. That if I was smart enough, I only had to rely on myself." He remembered the pain of those days. The mother who had abandoned him but whom he'd loved and wished would return. At first he hadn't wanted anyone to adopt him because he'd been sure his mother would come back for him.

When he'd realized she wouldn't, his anger had grown.

Classic behavior, he understood now.

"But everyone relies on you," Kate insisted. "Who helps *you*?"

"I don't need anyone. I'm happy as I am." For more than twenty years that had been his philosophy. Before he met Kate, he hadn't questioned it.

"But—" Another excruciating pain doubled her over and Kate fought for breath. Her hair matted to the back of her neck.

"We're almost there," Robert said.

Kate bit her lip again and thought about Robert's words. She knew he'd said them to distract her, but that didn't change how sad they were. "That's why you think what I'm doing, having a baby by myself, is wrong."

"Yes."

"But not every woman is like your mother."

Robert changed lanes and shot past another car. Where was the damn hospital? "Intellectually I understand that, Kate. You're not a drunk and you're financially secure. But you're still not giving your baby everything—a family. What if something happens to you? Oh, God, I'm sorry, I didn't mean it."

"There, Devlin. Turn there, that's the emergency wing."

Devlin stopped the car in front of the emergency doors. He turned to her, "Kate, I'm sorry for what I said. It was stupid."

"Oh, Devlin." She touched his face. "To think I once thought you were coldhearted. I know you didn't mean anything." Another pain hit her and she gasped. Devlin immediately swept her into his arms.

As soon as he carried Kate through the automatic doors, the emergency team swung into action and took her away from him. He filled out her forms, but as he wasn't family they wouldn't let him into the examination room with her.

Instead, he paced and worried. Nothing was going to happen to Kate or the baby, he assured himself. It could be one of a million things. He ran through the list of minor problems he'd heard about.

But she'd looked so scared when she'd left him.

Sweet, pretty Kate. Nothing could happen to her.

After an hour, Robert couldn't wait any longer and went in search of her. One examining room was empty, one held a very old man. In the third he found Kate.

"Devlin," she called when he entered the room. She burst into tears.

He took her hand and raised it to his lips, murmuring, "Katie, oh, sweetheart."

She raised a tear-stained face to him. "It's going to be okay. I didn't lose the baby."

THE NEXT MORNING, Robert was at the hospital as soon as visiting hours began. Juggling flowers, chocolates and a large stuffed animal as he walked into her private room, at first he didn't see that she was asleep. He made too much noise trying to find a place for the parcels and Kate stirred.

"What's all that?" she asked groggily and smiled at him.

Robert felt her smile all the way to his soul and wondered how Todd could have ever given that up. Todd Miller was clearly a complete and utter idiot.

"I'm sorry, I didn't mean to wake you," he said. Some of the color had returned to her face. Kate looked utterly beautiful.

He pulled a chair closer to her bed, sat down and took her hand. He realized he was using any excuse he could to touch her, but he didn't stop himself. "You scared me yesterday."

"I scared myself," Kate admitted. "But the doctor said it was only false labor pains."

"Which were probably caused by stress," he finished. Kate remained silent but she wouldn't meet his eyes. "Kate, you've been working too hard. You can't go back to work."

"Of course I can," she retorted. "Now you're going to tell me it's all my fault because I'm doing this on my own." Tears welled up in her eyes.

"Kate, please, that's not what I meant." Awkwardly, Robert stroked her hair, desperately wanting to calm her down. Being upset couldn't be good for her or the baby. "Sweetheart, the doctor said you needed bed rest until the birth."

"How can I do that?" Kate sniffed and wiped her eyes. "The campaign for Boardroom Baby and—what did you call me?"

Cursing his little slip of the tongue, Devlin said, "I'll coordinate the campaign. We'll turn your apartment into headquarters if you want, but you're only going to hear what we're doing and boss us around. No work yourself."

"Yes, sir." She smiled weakly and then fidgeted with her hands. "Do you call every woman you rescue 'sweetheart'?"

"Yes," he answered uncomfortably, his pulse speeding up. He was afraid she'd continue probing him but, luckily, the doctor entered.

"Dr. Jorgenson," she introduced him to Devlin.

Dr. Jorgenson nodded at Devlin, saying to Kate, "We met last night when your young man wouldn't go home until I promised him that you and the baby would be okay without him for twelve hours."

Robert felt himself flush but he met Kate's gaze. She winked at him.

The doctor examined her chart. "Everything checks out. As long as you promise to get lots of rest, I can let you go home tomorrow." He turned to Devlin. "Make sure she follows my orders."

Robert nodded, not trusting his voice. Kate and the baby would be all right.

The doctor flipped to the last page and frowned, then regarded Devlin. "Can you come back tomorrow for a blood test?"

"Me?" Devlin said.

"Why him?" Kate asked.

Dr. Jorgenson looked confused. "I'm sorry if I made a mistake—I thought you were the father." He shook his head. "I'm only fifty, but sometimes I'm out of step with the times." He turned to Kate. "The lab did tests on the baby and they'd like to confirm with the father's DNA. It's nothing serious. We'd just like to know for sure."

"Kate used a sperm donor," Robert said.

"Oh, of course. Well, then, check with your clinic. Some clinics have methods of getting in touch with the donor, others don't."

At Kate's white, shocked face, Robert took her hand again and squeezed. "What if the clinic can't get in touch with the donor?"

"It's not a big problem. We'll check the baby when it's six months old. Testing the father gives the answer faster." The doctor closed the chart. "It's highly unlikely to be a problem."

"I'll check with the clinic," Kate managed to croak. She felt hot and cold and nervous and glad that Devlin was holding on to her.

As the doctor left, Devlin took both her hands in his and rubbed them. "Kate, don't worry. It's not a real problem. I'm sure the clinic can get in touch with the donor and he'll agree to the test. It's minor." Kate remained silent and Devlin rambled, "Really nothing to worry about. Small chance there's any problem." Kate barely heard him.

She wanted him to know. She wanted him to share in her joy and her worries. Later she would blame it on hysteria but at that moment she wanted to set free what she'd had to keep caged in her mind all this time.

"I don't have to go to the clinic," she said.

"Kate, you have to. We need to check this out."

"I don't have to go to the clinic," she continued very calmly, "because I know who the father is."

Their eyes met and held for a long moment and Robert knew the words before she said them.

"You're the father of my baby, Robert Devlin."

10

ROBERT WHEELED Kate out of the hospital to his car without saying a word. In fact, he'd remained completely impassive. She'd only experienced his brief flare of anger yesterday as he'd stormed out of her room after her announcement about his impending fatherhood. Fine, two could play that game. "You didn't have to pick me up," she grumbled.

"I was here for the blood test, anyway."

"This chair is so ridiculous," she continued complaining and then stopped in confusion. Robert had halted in front of a minivan. A large, sedate brown van. "Where's your car?" she demanded.

"In my garage," he answered, but he didn't look at her. Instead, he opened the van's door and helped her inside. Kate waited until he'd made his way around to the driver's side. "Where did you get this...this suburban monstrosity?"

"From a dealership." He started the offending vehicle, checked all the mirrors and drove out of the parking lot. What was he thinking, driving such a fatherly kind of car? Did that mean he was happy about the news? She sneaked a quick peak at him, but the angry slash of his mouth certainly didn't indicate joy. Her momentary hope died.

Well, that was just fine. In typical Robert Devlin fashion he was planning to take control over her life. Well, she would just see about that! She was perfectly capable of looking after herself, by herself.

"Well?" Kate insisted.

"Well, what?"

The man was so infuriating! He knew very well what! Kate wished she were in her office where she could stomp her foot and still be in control. How had events ever gotten so past her?

"Why are you driving a van? It doesn't suit your style," she said tightly.

Robert shot her a bland look—the first time he'd really looked at her since her announcement yesterday—and then returned his attention to the road. "A van seemed more practical," he answered noncommittally.

Kate waited for him to say something more but he didn't. She knew he was angry and upset, but all he'd done after she'd dropped her bombshell was run out of her hospital room. She couldn't believe he'd just left her. All alone. And then he'd arrived this morning to take her home. As if nothing had happened!

Well Mr. Robert Devlin wasn't going to get away with that.

"No wonder no woman's wanted to marry you," she snapped. After she told him the truth, she'd imagined him shocked but happy. The three of them becoming a family...

"I said I'd never *asked* any woman to marry me. I have no idea if anyone ever wanted to."

"Trust me, no one did if this is how you treat your relationships."

"But we don't have a relationship," Devlin retorted, his lips tight.

"We have a child."

"Yes." He turned right onto the access route to her condominium, saying nothing more.

"Say something," Kate demanded after the silence stretched.

"You know my feelings on the subject of single-parent families. I think you're setting up this child for a lot of heartache."

"Well, like it or not, the deed is done. With your help, I might add."

Robert's shoulders stiffened. "I thought I was helping a couple, a real family, not some egocentric, selfish woman who values herself more than her baby!"

"How dare you!"

Robert slammed on the brakes and pulled into her parking lot. Kate threw her arm out onto the dash but the seat belt held her back. Noticing her actions, Devlin blanched. "Oh, God, I'm sorry. Is everything okay?"

That made her even angrier. Clearly, all Devlin cared about was the baby. Do-the-right-thing Devlin didn't care about her. All those pretty fantasies she'd been having about him, about *them*, were delusions. She unsnapped her seat belt but the van door wouldn't budge. Robert got out of the vehicle and opened it for her.

Kate stepped out of the van, ignoring Robert's hand. "I hate vans," she announced and hurried toward the door of the building. By the time she'd assured Joe she was fine, Devlin was behind her. She continued to ignore him as they got into the elevator together. She stared at the red lights as they counted the floors. Out of the corner of her eye she could see Devlin stone-faced beside her, but neither of them said a word.

When the elevator opened on her floor, she stomped down the hallway to her door. She turned to tell Devlin to leave, when he asked, "How long have you known I'm the father?"

That stopped her. She remembered how stunned she'd felt when she'd first learned the truth and she realized she owed Devlin an explanation. Maybe his disappearing trick yesterday was due to surprise, not disapproval. It was curious how much his approval mattered to her. Whatever it was that she felt for him, it was more than mere sexual attraction.

She unlocked the door and motioned for him to enter. Somehow Devlin managed to help her off with her coat without touching her.

"Do you want something?" she asked nervously. "Coffee, juice?"

"I'll get us some water." He pointed to the couch. "The doctor wants you to rest, so sit. Have you phoned your own doctor yet?"

"Yes, I have an appointment with Ellen first thing tomorrow, but I'm fine. Really," she added when it looked like he didn't believe a word she'd said.

"I'll drive you," Devlin said.

"You don't have to look after me," Kate protested.

"Yes, I do. I'm involved."

"Oh." He was right. Now that she'd told him about the baby, he *was* involved. And wasn't that what she'd wanted? Kate sighed. When had everything become so complicated? Why did she want Devlin with her when he wasn't around and then do nothing but fight when he was with her?

"Sit," he ordered again and for once she obeyed. She hated to admit it, but she was tired—and that was from one little car ride! Heavens, what was she in for?

"How do you know that it's me?" Devlin was studying the ravine through the window, his back to her.

Kate shifted uncomfortably, not wanting to admit to him how, once again, she had ignored the rules. But she didn't have a choice. "I broke into the clinic's computer system so I could find out who the father of my baby was."

"But the whole point of using an anonymous sperm donor was so that you wouldn't know." His voice remained detached as he continued to talk to the window.

"Yes. I thought that was a good idea...at first. But once I began to feel my baby move inside me, to really know I was going to be a mother, I had so many questions. I needed to know what kind of man the father was."

Now Devlin turned to look at her and shook his head. "That is so like you. The rules don't apply to Kate Ross. What were you planning to do once you found out his identity?"

"Nothing." At his pointed stare, she flushed. "All right, I just wanted to find him. But I wasn't going to disturb his life or anything. I just wanted to know something about him that I could tell our child."

"Instead of some paragon of a mystery man, you learned it was me."

"Yes." Her voice was so quiet she could barely hear it.

"That must have disappointed you."

"Not at all! Devlin, I admit I was shocked. I could never have imagined that it was you...but once I found out, I was happy."

Devlin could not believe her words. *Happy*. Obviously she was lying, trying to soothe his feelings. He needed to prove to her that it didn't matter to him. That he would be a terrible father.

"And what do you expect me to do now?" he asked in his coldest voice. "Marry you?"

Kate looked shocked. "Oh, no. I realize you don't approve of my actions, Robert." She pleated her skirt with her fingers. "There's no reason for you to. And now that you've had the test, there's nothing else I want to ask from you." She took a deep breath. "But I do want to tell you one thing. I will be a very good mother."

He was so angry and he could barely understand why. Kate wanted absolutely nothing from him. He should be glad. Hadn't he made that clear that he wasn't willing to give anything? That it would be a mistake for him to be involved? It wouldn't take Kate long to realize that it was a mistake for him to try to belong. She'd quickly realize he was a bad father. A bad husband.

He felt like running out of her apartment and escaping. Quitting Carlyle Industries and leaving. A desert island or a jungle sounded just about right.

But he wouldn't. He'd do what he could for Kate and the baby, until she grew tired of him.

God, how had he gotten into such a mess? He'd tried so hard to stay away from any kind of emotional commitments, and except for the Blackwoods, he'd succeeded perfectly. How had Kate Ross ruined all of his plans with one careless, irresponsible action?

But that was her. Impulsive, determined. And so very very beautiful.

She was also the mother of his child.

The idea was still incomprehensible. Ever since he'd learned that Kate had used the same infertility clinic that he'd used, he'd wondered. But the idea that they would be parents together was only fantasy, a pleasant delusion he had considered late at night when it was just him and his dreams. When no one could ever know.

But for it to really become true...

That was why he had fled the hospital yesterday. He'd been afraid of what he might do. Not because he'd been angry—he'd managed to manufacture that emotion for today so that Kate wouldn't suspect how happy he was.

Despite everything he knew about himself, he was determined to try to be a good father. He knew he was contradicting himself, but he couldn't help it. If loving the child was enough, then he could pull it off. Because he could love the baby—hell, he already loved it. A little boy or girl to hold his hand and ask questions. Who would need him. Whom he could love unconditionally.

Robert sank into what Kate was beginning to think of as his chair. She watched him for a while, wondering what was going on in that complicated mind of his. Did he really hate the idea of being a father so much?

She remembered how good he'd been with his godson. Clearly, Robert liked children. And the minivan. He'd bought it—so it meant he planned to be involved. Maybe things weren't so bleak, after all. She perked up.

And then deflated when she thought that maybe Robert had nothing against being a *father*. Maybe he really, really didn't like *her*.

But he'd kissed her.

So what, Kate rationalized. Men kissed women all the time and it didn't mean anything. He'd never followed up.

But he was concerned for her.

He was concerned for everyone. He probably knew more about her doorman than she did. "How's Joe's son?" she asked, to test her thesis.

"He's better since he transferred to that new school." Devlin didn't look up from his hands as he answered automatically.

"A school with special classes for the disabled."

"Yes."

"A school you happened to know about?" Kate concluded.

Devlin looked at her, puzzled. "Yes."

"Good heavens, Robert, is there anyone you don't help?"

"What's wrong with—"

"Nothing, absolutely nothing's wrong with being a Good Samaritan." Kate didn't know how to explain that she wanted to know he was helping her because he liked her—not because it was what he did. Trust her luck to become involved with a man destined for sainthood.

She considered what to do.

Devlin considered what to do.

She could make him leave her alone—except she didn't want him to.

He could tell her he had no interest in Kate or the baby—except it was a lie.

She could give him visitation rights—except she wanted to be with him, too.

He could ask for visitation rights—except he wanted to spend time with Kate as a family.

What she really wanted was for them to be a family.

What he really wanted was for them to be a family.

They both sat bolt upright.

"What?" Kate asked.

"Nothing."

He looked odd, as if something unpleasant had occurred to him. Kate ran a hand through her hair, hardly able to believe the conclusion she'd reached. What did she mean by this? Sure, she was attracted to Devlin, but that was a hormonal thing and should pass, shouldn't it? She'd been fantasizing about him a lot, but that was only because she'd been celibate for too long.

All she needed to do was get Devlin into her bed and then she'd get him out of her system.

Oh, sure. She looked down at her swelling stomach, she was a real femme fatale. All she'd have to do was put on her come-hither smile and he'd jump her. She laughed to herself at her delusions.

Devlin jumped at the look on Kate's face. If her lips held that mysterious sexy smile any longer, he wouldn't be able to control himself. He'd be on top of her and then... Devlin shook himself. His sexual fantasies about Kate were getting out of control. He'd always been able to keep a rigid check on himself before. All this situation required was some self-discipline. And a lot of cold showers.

Okay, so she found Devlin sexually desirable. She was a woman and what woman wouldn't? Kate concluded. And she'd learned there was a lot more to him than his stuffy image portrayed. She, who had thought herself so good at analyzing people, had been fooled. But now that she knew the real man, she liked him. And respected him. If she had to fill out a magazine survey about the perfect man, it would be Devlin.

But that didn't mean she loved him.

The worst thing was he now liked Kate. Sex he could get over. But her way of living life—of attacking and experiencing it, her determination to change outdated rules, to make everything better—was so different from his and so appealing. He'd been wrong in his initial assessment of her.

But that didn't mean he loved her.

She couldn't be in love with Devlin, Kate argued

with herself. It was utterly inconceivable. They were far too different. She was only having warm, fuzzy feelings toward him because of the baby. She was not in love with Robert Devlin.

Because he was incapable of falling in love. After thirty-eight years he knew that. Just because his pulse raced every time she entered a room, just because he counted minutes until he would see her again, just because he loved everything about her, didn't mean he loved her.

She was in love with Robert Devlin. Kate couldn't believe it!

He was in love with Kate Ross.

A knock at the door saved him. "I'll get it," Devlin said and rose without looking at Kate. As soon as he let in whoever was at the door, he had to get out of here or else he was going to do something very stupid like tell Kate—"Gina."

"Robert." Gina smiled warmly.

He looked surprised but held the door open for her as she was balancing a pile of binders. "Come in." He grabbed the top green binder that looked about to topple off. "This way." He pointed to Kate's dining-room table.

Kate wished she were a better person and not resentful of how happy Robert had looked to see Gina. Or how natural the two of them looked together. Or to feel jealous at how svelte Gina looked in black leggings and a red sweater.

Gina carefully deposited the rest of the material on

the table and looked around in appreciation. "Your apartment is beautiful, Kate. So warm and homey."

Sourly, Kate wondered if this was said in surprise. *Stop being so mean-spirited*, she reminded herself. Her hormones were no excuse. It was jealousy, pure and simple. Although there was nothing pure and simple about it.

But what was Gina doing here?

Gina had turned to Robert. "I checked my voice mail and received your instructions about setting up headquarters in Kate's home."

"I meant for you to do that on Monday, Gina. Today is for your family."

"The kids are spending the day with my parents, anyway, so I was planning to work. I figured you'd be here so I thought we could get a head start. Is the kitchen over there? I'll make some coffee." Gina was halfway across the living room when she stopped. Looking awkward, she turned toward Kate. "I was sorry to hear you had a bad scare. I'm sure everything will be all right and I want you to know I'm here to help as much as I can. No way will the men at Carlyle be able to use this against you. Not meaning Mr. Devlin, of course," Gina added with a fond look in his direction.

"Of course," Kate said weakly. Devlin sure did inspire devotion, she mused. But as Gina disappeared into the kitchen, she recalled what the woman had said about the pregnancy. She turned on him.

"You didn't tell her, did you?"

"Tell her what?" Robert raised his head from a print-out.

"About the baby and...you," she faltered, regretting her words as Robert took off his glasses and glared at her.

"Don't be ridiculous," he snapped. "I've barely had time to digest the news. I hardly want to spread the story throughout Carlyle Industries."

"Oh, of course not," Kate agreed, telling herself to just shut up. She'd thought Robert might have told Gina because of their relationship but realized that what he'd said was right. Robert had only learned he was the father of Kate's baby twenty-four hours ago. He was still coming to terms with the fact. He probably hadn't even considered what the announcement would do to his and Gina's relationship.

She hoped the news ended their affair.

Damn, she wasn't that small-minded and selfish, was she? She wanted Robert to be happy, didn't she?

Yes.

But she wanted him to be happy with her.

Obviously she was selfish and small-minded.

So what.

She wanted Robert.

The doorbell rang. Before Kate or Robert had a chance to move a muscle, Gina set down the coffee tray and headed to the door.

She let in Ted Kenton, a junior account executive on Robert's team. "Picked up my voice mail and got your message, Gina." He smiled broadly at her. "Thought we might as well get started today." He carried in

some videotapes. "I've got the rough cuts of the commercials."

"Ted, that's wonderful," Gina said. "But how did
you get them today?"

"Told our ad guy it's an emergency—which it is—
and he owed me."

The doorbell rang once more. By the time Gina had
let in Linda Shaw, Art Mandelson, Feroze Sumatra, So-
phie Dimitris and Jason Blake, all members of Robert's
team, Kate realized she had underestimated him yet
again.

She knew her team members liked working for her,
but she didn't inspire the same loyalty that Robert did.
She realized that if she probed any one of them she
would learn what extraordinary feat or favor Robert
had done for each of them.

And now they were returning the favor and helping
her.

As command central formed before her, Kate had an
overwhelming urge to cry. In fact, she thought she
might, and as she heard the doorbell ring yet again, she
quietly sneaked out of the living room into her bedroom.

She fought back her tears and tore apart a tissue,
then she tore apart another tissue.

Pull yourself together, Ross, she told herself firmly.

She had so many things to be happy about.

First and foremost and always, the baby.

She was going to have a sweet-smelling, soft little
baby. She was going to be a mother.

She had great colleagues helping her put together a baby-food campaign in record time.

She had Robert Devlin.

No, that wasn't true. He was the father of her baby—which thrilled her—but he had no feelings for her.

And she wanted him to!

Oh, how she wanted...

"Kate?" Robert asked from the doorway.

Quickly, she wiped her eyes and composed her voice. "I'll be right out. I just needed a few minutes to myself."

Robert crossed the room in a few long strides. He sat next to her on the bed and took her hands in his. "I'm sorry about all the people out there. It seems to be a habit we've gotten into."

"You mean your team frequently appears on a Sunday out of the blue to work on a problem?"

"It's happened before," he admitted. "But this is bad timing. You're just home from the hospital and need to rest."

"I'm not an invalid," she insisted, removing her hand from his. She felt lonely without him touching her but she didn't want his sympathy. She didn't want Robert Devlin, Super Boss and friend to all, looking after her like he did everyone else.

She wanted him to think of her as a woman.

"Kate, we need to talk about the baby."

Unfortunately, the only manner in which Devlin thought of her was as the incubator for his sperm. Or maybe *accelerator* was the correct scientific term.

"There's nothing to talk about," she said. "I'm sorry

I told you. You needn't worry that I'm about to make any claims on you or want you as part of my baby's life. As soon as the baby-food campaign is over, I won't bother you again. We'll go back to how we were before." She didn't dare look at him as she waited for him to say that wasn't what he wanted. That he wanted to be involved with her. That he cared for her. Anything.

"Robert, did you want to use the film footage of the Cincinnati woman or the Saint Louis woman?" Gina asked from the doorway and then blinked at the cozy picture the pair made.

"Cincinnati," Kate said.

"Saint Louis," Robert answered.

Kate knew that Robert wasn't going to say the words she longed to hear. Her emotional life might be out of control, but she could still be in charge when it came to business.

Kate stood and marched toward the door. "Saint Louis is all wrong," she said disdainfully. "I'd better see to this."

Robert shook his head, muttering, "Doesn't know what she's talking about," and exited past Gina.

Gina sighed.

Days passed in a blur of meetings. It seemed that almost as soon as she got up in the morning, someone, usually Gina, was at her door with the newest set of memos, production figures and advertising materials.

The day continued with a series of people and emergencies in and out of her apartment. There weren't any more leaks to Grannie Goodspoon. But everyone remained on edge. Gina complained that she'd caught her boss reading through her Boardroom Baby notes. Jennifer said she never let any important documents out of her sight. Devlin, too, was a frequent visitor, but he kept their relationship strictly professional.

Twice she had caught him staring at her and her expanding middle with a look of bemused wonder. It had given her hope through all the days when they didn't say one personal word to each other.

Hadn't he felt anything when he'd kissed her? She'd been sure he had, had been sure he felt the same hunger and need she'd experienced, but Devlin never said a word. Or made any excuses to touch her. Or looked at her in any way except purely professionally.

Kate sighed. She really wished he cared for her.

It hurt that he didn't.

The only personal question he had asked was about the baby and his blood test, which had been negative, as the doctor had predicted. Their baby was healthy.

She was mere days away from her due date and desperately in love with the man who had fathered her baby.

You really did have to be careful what you wished for.

11

"BABY LOVE."

"Baby Time For Daddy," Phil Jones suggested as a slogan.

Kate leaned back in her chair and smiled contentedly. Her baby did a swan dive. Definitely a 7.6. She wondered if their child would be athletic. Physical skills would have to come from Robert. She had never been any good at sports, and since she liked to win she hadn't pursued them any further.

It was time she learned how to play just for fun—she wanted to share that with her child. Maybe Robert could help her with that.

Kate snapped herself out of her daydream. She'd read the books. Her fantasies were supposed to center exclusively on the baby. But Robert drew her attention as though he were a magnet and she was solid steel, instead of a fat and bloated female.

She hoped Gina appreciated him.

To distract herself she went into the kitchen for a glass of orange juice.

And found Gina kissing Ted Kenton.

Kate was so shocked that she just stood there gaping. Finally, Gina noticed Kate and broke away from Ted.

"Oh, Ms. Ross," she gasped and straightened her hair. "I, we, er—"

"Yes, I could see what you were doing," Kate said dryly. And then she couldn't contain her anger. This woman was involved with Robert. How could she betray him like this? Were there more Teds somewhere in the background? "How could you, Gina?"

Gina raised her chin under Kate's fierce scowl. "We weren't doing anything wrong, Kate."

Kate acknowledged the gauntlet of equality thrown at her with Gina's use of her first name. Gina had more than proven her worth during the campaign and she wouldn't cower under Kate's anger just because Kate was her superior in the office. Kate turned her attention to Ted. "If you could leave us alone for a minute." She nodded toward the door.

Ted looked hesitant but Gina nodded at him and he left.

"He's a very handsome man," Kate commented. Was Gina really foolish enough to value Ted's boyish good looks more than Devlin's innumerable strengths? Robert was worth a thousand Teds!

"That's the one thing I held against Ted. My ex-husband was a very handsome man."

"What about Robert?" Kate couldn't face Gina so she began pacing the small kitchen.

"What about him?'

"Ted. Robert. How could you hurt him like this?"

"Ted hasn't got anything against Robert."

"He doesn't!" Kate squeaked and then stopped her

suspicious thoughts. Gina was not sleeping her way to the top. "Does Robert know about Ted?"

"No." Gina blushed.

"Don't you think you should tell him?"

"So soon? Ted and I, well, we didn't think it was a good idea to tell anyone about us until we'd been together longer. Till we knew whether or not it was going to work. You know what Carlyle is like about employees dating."

"Yes." Kate nodded and began to wonder if she'd completely misunderstood the situation. "What about Robert?" she asked again.

Enlightenment finally hit Gina. "But Robert and I aren't—"

"You're not?" Kate demanded eagerly.

"No. In fact, I thought you two…"

"Oh, no," Kate insisted, but she couldn't stop the little glow of happiness that lit itself inside her.

Robert and Gina were not a couple. Robert was a free man.

But then the hope was snuffed out when she realized that unlike her, Robert had known he was a free man.

Clearly, he wasn't interested.

ROBERT WONDERED what was taking Kate so long in the kitchen. Ted had come out looking kind of funny. Maybe he should go check. No, he was as much involved in Kate's life as he wanted to be.

Robert took off his glasses and rubbed the bridge of his nose. Funny, his eyewear had never bothered him before Kate became a part of his life.

He looked at the kitchen door again, but still no Gina or Kate.

He wished he had the right to ask Kate what was wrong. Sometimes he caught her looking at Gina with the most peculiar expression on her face.

But he didn't have the right.

He could still hear Kate's words very clearly. He wasn't to be part of her little family.

He should concentrate on what he knew: business. Finding out who was betraying Carlyle Industries. But for once in his life, work wasn't his first priority. He found himself daydreaming about all kinds of possibilities. All centering around Kate and the baby. Which was ridiculous, he reminded himself once again. Kate was mildly interested in him at the moment because he was the father of her child. And because they had been thrown together so much. But soon she would lose interest; they always did. She'd find out about the real him and leave. Leave his life. Leave him alone.

And for the first time in a long time, that idea bothered Robert a lot.

Finally, Kate entered the living room but she, too, looked peculiar. Trying to figure out what was going on, Robert examined the room and had to admit it didn't much look like her cozy apartment any longer. Instead, boxes of files overflowed, laptop computers covered the surface areas of tables and several large pieces of cardboard were tacked onto her dining-room walls. Robert wondered how the boards had been attached to the walls and if they could be removed without tearing off the wallpaper. Knowing the occasionally careless enthusiasm of this group, he rather doubted Kate's apartment would be left unscathed.

Kate glanced at him and then sat in the armchair Ted vacated for her. She looked glorious. It had to be the green of her sweater that put the sparkle in her eyes. And pregnant women did glow. Kate looked as if she'd just been handed a coveted prize.

Their child. His and Kate's.

He had never said the words out loud but he had mentally tried them out many times. He'd considered telling her how he felt, but he was afraid of being rejected outright. No, a better plan was to work slowly. To get himself more and more involved with Kate's life. Then he might be able to win her over. He saw Kate move to sit next to Jennifer, who was observing him. Looking away quickly, he rejoined the group watching the final Boardroom Baby commercials. As much as he tried to overhear what Kate and Jennifer were discussing, he couldn't.

Jennifer leaned over to whisper to Kate. "Boardroom Baby seems under complete control. It's going to launch the day before Grannie's." Her eyes scanned the group. "Whoever has been feeding them information has stopped now that the heat's on." She elbowed Kate gently in the side. "Now, why do you look like the cat who swallowed the canary? Does it have to do with Devlin? When he thinks no one notices he observes you."

"He does?" The idea warmed Kate.

"Does he know?" Jennifer suddenly asked.

"Yes. Don't you think he's perfect?"

"As a father for your baby or a man for you?"

"Both."

Jennifer looked at her critically. "Kate, be careful. You sound as infatuated as a schoolgirl."

"I am." Kate giggled.

"Kate—"

"I know I'm being silly. But I have this feeling that maybe I can have it all."

"Kate, be careful. Emotions can turn on you, not make you think clearly. Are you sure you care for him and not just who he is?"

"Director of marketing, Eastern Division?"

"The father of your child."

"It's like fate, like we were meant to be together." Kate knew she wouldn't be able to convince Jennifer that what she felt for Robert was right. She was willing to risk being hurt, especially now that she knew he was a free man.

But she couldn't think about that now because she felt something...weird happen in her lower body, just as it had earlier in the kitchen. She'd been too busy talking to Gina to give the strange sensation any thought, but now she wondered... Could that have been a contraction? If so, it wasn't nearly as bad as she'd feared. Of course, it was only the beginning. A great sense of delight filled her. Imagine, the moment was almost here. Her dream coming true. No matter what the future held for her and Devlin, soon she would be a mother! She leaned closer to Jennifer and beamed at her friend. "I think that was a contraction."

Jennifer jumped as if she'd had a contraction herself.

Kate touched her arm. "Relax. First I need to have another contraction and then we'll time them. It could be a false alarm."

Two hours later Kate knew it was the real thing. The contractions had moved from every twenty minutes to fifteen minutes apart. The strength and pain of the contractions had also been steadily increasing. Kate didn't know how long she had been walking the room, rubbing her back, but it seemed to help. It also took her mind off what was ahead. She was glad Jennifer had paid attention in the childbirth classes; she didn't think she could do this alone.

Luckily, the Boardroom Baby team was so busy putting the final touches onto the campaign no one had noticed Kate's odd behavior. Not even Devlin, who was usually so observant. Everyone probably thought that Kate was pacing out of nervousness. After all, Boardroom Baby was her baby.

There was still a part of her that could barely believe she really was going to be a mother; a bigger part of her was more than a little scared. She was glad Jennifer would be with her even if her friend did look very pale. Kate squeezed her hand reassuringly.

"Kate, I don't know if I can do this," Jennifer said between clenched lips.

"Of course you can, " Kate insisted, but she was worried, too. Jennifer had gotten very faint during the childbirth video and Kate had left the room with her for a drink of water. What if they had missed something really important? Like the secret to controlling pain? she wondered as another pain, stronger yet, overtook her.

It was time.

She might be scared, Kate told herself, but she could do this. Millions of women had given birth. It was natural.

None of those thoughts reassured her.

Then she thought, Robert is the father of my child. That made her feel strong. Now she could do anything. Even natural childbirth—maybe.

Robert was wrapping up his thank-you speech announcing that Boardroom Baby would begin shipping tomorrow. They had signed off on the film for the magazine and newspaper ads. Everything was ready. She was glad her baby was showing such impeccable timing. But she really shouldn't expect less from Robert's baby.

Robert finished and looked toward Kate. She nodded and struggled toward the group seated around her dining-room table. "I share every sentiment Robert expressed. Your energy, devotion and commitment are what made Boardroom Baby happen." She glanced at Devlin. "As well, I'd like to thank Robert for everything." She flinched involuntarily at another labor pain and Robert frowned. "I know I've learned about teamwork from you. Oh—" That really hurt.

"Kate, was that the same contraction or a separate one?" Jennifer demanded.

Kate panted, trying to draw in breath as her childbirth instructor had taught her. She wished it had more effect. "I've never done this before so I'm not sure, but

I think it was the same." At another contraction, she sat on the couch. "Then again, maybe they're different. No matter what, I think we should go to the hospital. Boardroom Baby is about to have its first customer!"

ROBERT PACED the hospital waiting room, impatient for news about Kate, for the second time in his life. He wished that he, too, could be in the delivery room and decided to hell with waiting for an invitation.

He went down the hall toward Kate's room, stopping at a supply cupboard to don the gown and cap he'd seen all the other expectant fathers wearing. *All the other expectant fathers.* He liked the sound of that.

As he entered the room, the doctor was finishing her examination of Kate. "You're eight centimeters dilated. It won't be much longer," Dr. Chase announced.

"Can't you hurry it up?" a pale Jennifer asked. "I'm not sure how much more—" Kate interrupted her with a moan and grabbed Jennifer's hand and squeezed hard.

After half a minute or so, the labor pain passed and Kate raised her exhausted face, saw Robert and smiled.

"Kate." He was incapable of saying anything else. She looked so beautiful.

"Robert, I'm glad you're here!" said Jennifer, rubbing her sore hand.

"Ellen, this is Robert Devlin, my—"

"Colleague from work," he filled in, still riding that bubble of pleasure from Kate's clear happiness at seeing him.

"Thank God you're here," Jennifer added, sounding

strange. She looked paler than Kate and wiped the sweat off her own forehead. As another contraction started, Kate grabbed Jennifer's hand once again. Jennifer looked pleadingly at him.

"Robert, can you take over and help Kate? I need to get some fresh air."

Robert took Kate's hand as Jennifer left the room. She squeezed it tightly as another pain hit her. He counted her through her breathing exercise and then offered her the paper cup of ice chips. "Thanks." She smiled through her exhaustion. "I'm so glad you're here, Robert. I really need you."

"You're doing great," he reassured.

"I must look awful," she insisted, and Robert was glad that she was fishing for a compliment. The obvious pain Kate was experiencing scared him; he wished he could do something for her.

"You look beautiful." Unable to help himself, he raised her hand to his lips to kiss the back, and then turned her small, gentle hand over to kiss the palm.

"Robert, I'm sorry I dragged you into this. That I broke the rules and found out you were the baby's father. It was wrong of me."

"Don't say that, Kate. Your baby, you, are the best things that have ever happened to me."

Kate wanted to tell him how she felt, but another contraction took over. The next hours passed in a blur—Robert massaging her back, her shoulders. Robert holding her hand and telling her over and over that she was doing great, that it would be over soon. At first Kate had been able to tease him about how much he knew about childbirth—and extracted a reluctant admission that he'd read about childbirth and rented a video.

But after a while, Kate lost herself in a haze of pain and waiting, of nurses and doctors arriving to check on her progress. What she held on to, literally and figuratively, was Robert. *His* strength brought her through, *his* voice was the one she heard telling her to push hard one last time.

At last, she heard the baby cry and Robert whispered, "It's a girl. We have a daughter."

"Of course it's a girl," Kate grumbled. "I told everyone it would be." But he'd said the most beautiful words, the ones she'd dreamed about. We have a daughter. *We.*

"We're a family," she whispered very quietly to her little daughter, Sarah. And hoped that it was true.

12

LESS THAN THREE WEEKS LATER Kate wondered how she'd ever thought having it all would be easy. Okay, she'd never truly believed it would be *easy*, but she had thought it would be manageable.

The nanny, Katrin, was a big help, but Kate found every day so overwhelming. Of course, Carlyle Industries understood she was on maternity leave, but that hadn't stopped them from sending over one or two emergency projects for her to fill her time with.

Her parents had visited several times, but Kate reminded herself they had their own lives. Anne, too, had been over and had assured Kate that she'd get used to her new schedule. But it was Robert she relied on.

Boardroom Baby had hit the grocery-store shelves running. Carlyle could hardly keep up with orders. It seemed that nineties mothers were responding positively to Boardroom Baby's marketing strategy. Of course, they only had sales figures from a few target stores, but the sample group generally reflected the nation. Grannie Goodspoon, meanwhile, was lagging far behind.

Kate received daily reports from her colleagues at the office and even a couple of salespeople had phoned to gloat over how well Carlyle was performing. They'd shared a number of jokes about good ole Grannie being past her prime. She found the news gratifying, but her career was no longer her focus.

Anderson had even visited Kate at home. She didn't know who had been more uncomfortable by that visit; she in her sweat suit with her hair tied back in a ponytail, her feet bare, or Anderson in his navy pinstripes trying to avoid baby drool. Still, Kate appreciated the gesture and his news. He wasn't going to announce the vice presidency until Kate returned to work full-time. Which meant she had a really good shot. Which meant she had to return to work soon.

What she looked forward to every day was Robert's visits. He'd rearranged his schedule to arrive at her apartment by six o'clock to have dinner and visit with his daughter. As neither of them had really ever cooked before, they stumbled through several burnt and bizarre-tasting casseroles before Kate broke down and pulled out her credit card and her take-out list.

"You don't cook. I can't cook. This is ridiculous."

The doorbell rang and Kate wondered if it was Bruno's Fine Foods or Robert.

It was Bruno's.

Kate sighed and set the table. It was a cozy setup, all right, except for the fact that Robert barely acknowledged her.

The door opened—she'd given him his own set of keys, it seemed easier—and Robert came in. Looking tired.

"Long day?"

"Meetings, voice mail and E-mail—I didn't get to any of the projects I need to work on." He put his briefcase and keys on the hall table. Removing his glasses, he rubbed his forehead.

"You have a headache."

"No worse than usual. Is Sarah asleep?"

Kate shouldn't be jealous of her own daughter but she was. "She fell asleep an hour ago. We should get through dinner before she wakes up hungry. Here—" Kate helped Robert out of his suit jacket and led him to the couch "—sit for a minute and relax. You work too hard." She began to massage his shoulders and wondered about herself. *You work too hard.* When had she turned into June Cleaver? She should be worrying about the vice presidency, instead she wished he'd turn around and take her in his arms. Kiss her and tell her he'd missed her.

Forget it, Kate, she told herself. If Robert had felt anything substantial for her, he would have told her by now. After all, they had experienced the birth of their child together. No, he loved Sarah. He tolerated Kate.

Robert smelled baby powder and Kate's own seductive scent as her fingers pressed into his flesh. Relax, he told himself, it was just a massage. Kate didn't mean anything by it, she was just grateful. Nothing more.

She had no idea what her touch did to him. She had no idea that after he left her apartment, he drove to his place to take a very long and very cold shower.

It was why he kept himself so remote when he was around Kate and poured all of his passion into their little baby girl. He knew that Kate wondered about his actions, his aloofness, but he couldn't let it be any other way.

It was much safer to love Sarah.

He let himself enjoy the touch of Kate's hands on his skin for another minute and then he clamped down his self-control. He was famous for his self-control, he reminded himself. He stood. "I'm going to go check on Sarah." He left Kate sitting alone on the couch.

She looked hurt but he told himself it was better this way. For both of them.

ON SATURDAY her doorbell rang and Kate gladly put aside her files to answer it. Maybe Robert had forgotten his keys to her apartment and was returning early with Sarah. He'd taken their daughter out for some fresh air and to give Kate a chance to get caught up on her work. But she missed both of them already.

It was Anne. "But you don't get out on Saturdays," Kate exclaimed. With all the lessons Anne's kids took, Saturday was her busiest day.

"I thought you could maybe use a break." Anne breezed into the apartment. "Where's Sarah?"

Kate hadn't told anyone in her family about Robert—she didn't have the faintest idea how to describe what he was in her life—but she couldn't think of what else to say. Besides, this was her sister and she did want to tell Anne about Robert, so she blurted out, "Sarah is with Robert."

"Robert?" Anne teased gently. "Is he the darkly attractive man who coached you through your labor?"

"Yes. How did you know?"

"I asked one of the nurses. I had this suspicion you had a new man in your life, but after Todd, I knew you would be gun-shy about telling your family. You could have told me, Kate."

"Oh, I wanted to, Anne, but it's so complicated." Kate paced. "Robert is in my life, but not exactly in the way you imagine." She took a deep breath and turned to face her concerned sister. "Robert is Sarah's father."

"How? You went to a sperm bank. How can that be?"

Kate shrugged, hating to admit what she'd done. "You know me. Let nothing stop Kate Ross. I found out the name of my sperm donor."

Anne shook her head at Kate. "And then you went and knocked on this man's door and introduced yourself?"

"I wish it were only that simple! The father is Robert Devlin."

"Robert Devlin? Your archenemy, Robert Devlin? The evil, small-minded Robert Devlin?" Anne sat down on the couch.

Kate sat next to her, holding her sister's hand for reassurance. "I may have exaggerated Robert slightly. He's been just wonderful to me and Sarah. Everything is such a mess." To her horror, Kate burst into tears.

Anne gathered Kate into her arms, soothing her. Kate was glad to sob out the whole story: how she'd broken into the clinic computer; how she'd tried to keep the secret but, when the baby had been threatened, had told Robert; how he believed that raising a child alone was wrong.

Finally, Kate was able to stop her torrent of words and tears and she blew her nose. "Excuse me, I'm going to the bathroom to splash some water on my face."

When she came back into the living room, Anne was smiling. "I didn't think my predicament was funny at all," Kate complained.

"But it is, Kate," Anne assured her. "If you could only see yourself. Collected, always-sure-of-herself Kate Ross has finally been completely flummoxed by a man. I was beginning to think the day would never come."

"You don't have to sound so pleased about it."

Anne patted Kate's hand reassuringly. "I love you very much and I respect everything you've managed to accomplish in your career, but you've always been so good at everything, it's nice to find out you can be as insecure as the rest of us. Now, what are you doing about winning over Robert?"

"What do you mean?"

"Kate, you always, *always* have a plan of action for any problem that arises. You seem to think that Robert doesn't think of you as a woman. Has he ever kissed you?"

"Well..." Kate realized she was blushing. "Yes."

"A real kiss? One that made your toes curl?"

"Definitely."

"Then use sex," Kate's practical sister announced.

"Sex!" Kate squeaked out.

"Sex. Man, woman, physical intimacy. I know you had your baby the new-fashioned way, but you must know about sex."

Kate could hardly believe what Anne was advising. "Stop teasing. You think I should seduce Robert?"

"Definitely." Anne smiled widely. "Seducing our future husbands is a time-honored Ross-family tradition. David didn't realize how serious I was about him until after I had taken him to bed."

Kate considered Anne's advice. It wasn't like her to just let events happen out of her control. She should try to take control, show Robert how she felt about him. Then the meaning of Anne's words penetrated. "What did you mean by *tradition*?" she asked suspiciously.

"Who do you think taught me?" Anne responded. "Mom, of course."

ROBERT STEPPED OUTSIDE his front door, set the burglar alarms, locked the door and turned to find Kate. Her cheeks were pink-tipped, her eyes sparkling. She smiled at him with a smile that meant she was up to something.

"Sarah wanted to come see your home."

He noticed his daughter strapped in a baby carryall across Kate's chest. "Sarah does make her desires well known," he acknowledged.

Kate's smile got bigger and he felt himself melt. Ever since Sarah's birth he'd tried to build up his resistance to Kate, but it was no good. He was completely and utterly in love with her.

At least he was quite sure Kate didn't suspect. He hadn't allowed himself to let out the faintest hint of his true feelings.

The more he wanted to say, the more curt and

abrupt he became. Kate had only taken a month's maternity leave. For the past week since she'd returned to Carlyle part-time, he'd managed to avoid her almost completely. He'd offered to look after Sarah on the evenings Kate wanted to work late. They managed to share Sarah and see very little of each other.

Clearly, Kate wondered why and was about to tackle the lion in his den. He had to invite them inside but he hesitated. No one came to visit him at his home, not even Alan and his family. Once Kate and Sarah entered his house, they'd leave their mark. He wouldn't be able to look at any room without remembering Kate there.

He held open the door. "You might as well come in."

His voice was so curt that Kate was tempted to flee. This was a really bad idea. Obviously Robert was not happy to see her; he was only tolerating her.

She'd just stay a few minutes and then leave. Let Robert have his much-desired solitary existence. In a way, she was glad that he didn't pretend to be happy to see her. It was better that she knew where she stood. She would put herself and Robert back in a business relationship only. Sarah would be their sole connection. And the way Robert had carefully split the child-care responsibilities meant they never had to see each other.

She missed seeing him. Arguing with him. That was why she was humiliating herself at his house.

His home shocked her. The living room held only a dark brown couch, a brass coffee table and a large wall unit housing a television, VCR and CD system.

The dining room's mahogany table looked as if it had never been used. A room that was his office looked more full because of the bookshelves it contained, but there was nothing personal anywhere. No pictures or mementos, flowers or pillows to soften the strict utilitarian lines of the rooms.

It was as if no one lived here.

Kate stole a look at him but he remained impassive as she wandered through his home.

Home was the wrong word. It was more like an institution. Robert could walk away from this place tomorrow taking nothing with him and he'd be leaving nothing behind.

Why did he punish himself like this? Why didn't he make himself a place that was his?

Upstairs, the first room she checked was completely empty. The room next to it had to be the master bedroom but Kate couldn't face it. Instead, she noticed a closed door farther down the hall. As Kate walked toward it, she felt Robert flinch, and when she turned to him, she saw some kind of emotion cross his face. She was sorry she'd come here. She'd had all kinds of pleasant fantasies about Robert being excited to see her; about her and Sarah fitting into his home so well that he'd realize they should be together. She'd imagined the two of them bustling around in the kitchen, laughing, catching each other's eye... At the scowl on Robert's face, she stopped before the closed door and sighed.

She didn't want to see any more, but she forced herself to open one more door and stare at one more sterile, unlived-in environment.

Except this room was different.

It was Sarah's room.

Kate could only look around in amazement. The nursery was a hue of soft rainbow colors and decals of bunnies. "It's beautiful," she said.

Robert wouldn't meet her eyes. He walked across Sarah's room and looked out the window.

"I like the bunnies," Kate added, wishing he would talk to her. Why was he so willing to lavish love on Sarah but take none for himself?

"I thought the bunnies would make it seem more like home."

As if on cue, Sarah gurgled and waved her chubby little arms. "She likes her room," Kate said. She handed Sarah to Robert. "Why don't you have her try out her new crib."

Robert didn't say anything as he lay Sarah down. He touched her nose and then kissed it and Kate felt herself fall more and more in love with him. Sarah's room had given her new hope. Robert needed her and Sarah; he needed their love, whether he admitted it or not. She was going to prove it to him.

A man who could so lovingly decorate his daughter's room needed to be loved in return. But why did he turn such a stubborn eye toward her? He refused to acknowledge any more than some vestiges of sexual attraction between them.

He looked incredibly sexy putting his daughter to bed.

It brought all kinds of totally different bed images to mind.

Kate clamped down on her desires. She'd been having even more lustful thoughts than usual about Robert Devlin. She supposed it was only natural because it had been a long time since she'd last...well. Moreover, her figure was coming back and she felt attractive. She wanted Robert to look at her as a woman and not as the mother of his child. She'd dressed in a green sweater and black leggings hoping he'd appreciate her refound curves. So far, he hadn't even taken a look.

She needed to change that. She had to try. "Oh, look, you have baby monitors. Let's turn one on and let Sarah have a nap."

"Here? Now?"

"You did set up this room for her. Were you planning on having her stay over after she starts college?" Kate took his arm, glad for the excuse to touch him, and steered him out of the nursery. "See." She held up the monitor. "We'll hear the first peep she makes." She let her gaze rove over Devlin, from his toes, over his long hard body to his fiery dark eyes. She felt herself grow warm as she said, "The only room I haven't seen is your bedroom."

Robert told himself he was imagining things. He had not seen desire in Kate's face as she'd asked to see his bedroom. He was projecting his own want on to her. She looked so beautiful, in the soft green sweater brushing enticingly along all the curves he burned to touch.

Kate was only making conversation while he was making an ass of himself. He'd barely put a sentence together since she'd arrived on his doorstep.

As he'd looked at his house through her eyes, he'd

cringed. He'd expected her to voice disapproval, but she'd remained silent, looking at him more and more curiously.

Her home and his were polar opposites—and that was what he wanted, wasn't it? He wanted his address to be a place to sleep and keep his clothes, nothing more. Then he could leave at any time.

Why wasn't Kate saying anything?

The sooner he showed her everything—he knew her curiosity wouldn't let her leave until she'd seen every last nook and cranny—the sooner she would be gone.

Even as he led her down the corridor to his bedroom, he knew it was too late. Kate and Sarah were inextricably part of his life.

He, Robert Devlin, who had so carefully kept himself separate from the rest of the world, was caught, enmeshed by the messy, complicated life of a woman who was the opposite of everything that he was.

He wasn't sure exactly when he'd lost himself to her, but he had. And Sarah... There wasn't anything he wouldn't do for his daughter.

Who'd have ever believed his one good deed would reap him such rewards?

Devlin's bedroom was more like the man she had come to admire. It was plain, furnished in Robert's favorite dark woods, with blues and plaids, and the bed was large and comfortable. An overstuffed chair with a reading lamp was positioned under a window, disorganized pile of paperbacks on the floor next to it. Mystery and suspense covers that she recognized. A TV was angled for easy viewing from the bed.

Kate smiled. "Thank goodness I've found some human weaknesses, Devlin." She picked up one of the paperbacks and scanned the cover. She hadn't read it yet. Who'd have thought she and Devlin shared similar tastes in authors. "I was beginning to be afraid I might find your room as bare as a monk's cell. Or the walls covered with charts of everyone you planned to help arranged like battle plans."

"You make me sound like a Good Samaritan."

"You are, and more." Kate was nervous but she had to say what she felt. She wanted Devlin to think of her as a woman and not as another good-work project. "You're probably the best person I know." Robert actually blushed as Kate hurried on. "I admit that's not what I thought at first. I let myself believe what I wanted to believe—that you only cared about numbers. And getting ahead.

"The truth is that I was the one who was only interested in getting ahead." Robert looked as if he was about to say something but Kate held up her hand. "No, let me finish—apologies aren't easy for me. What I want to say is that I was wrong and you were right. And you've been nothing but a help ever since I've gotten you involved in my life. And it's the best thing that's ever happened to me." Now she dared to take a look at him, hoping he'd say he was happy, too. He didn't.

She pushed her hair back and continued. "I know that when you went to the clinic you were doing a good deed and you wanted anonymity. Instead, you got me and my messy life."

"I like being involved in your life," he said quietly.

She took a deep breath. "You love Sarah, but what about me?" There—she'd said it.

"You're a wonderful mother."

"I mean as a woman. Are you, do you..." He had to know what she meant. She chewed her lip nervously and dropped her eyes to the floor. Her courage fled and she searched for a distraction to get herself out of the situation. "You even dust under the bed!"

"I have a cleaner. Kate—" Somehow, Devlin had crossed the room and was standing in front of her. She was afraid to look at him, afraid to see his face and learn he didn't care about her. She finally knew what Todd had been talking about when he'd ended their engagement. About his desire for a great love. She didn't know how she could continue if Robert rejected her. She felt tears well up in her eyes and realized she was about to cry.

"Kate." Devlin's fingers touched her chin, raising her face, and he was shocked to see the moisture on her cheeks. "Kate, you have to know I would never do anything to hurt you." She tried to smile but her lips only trembled. He couldn't help himself as he drew her into his arms. She went willingly and wrapped her arms around his back.

She felt so soft and good and was everything he'd ever wanted and always denied himself.

He wasn't going to deny himself any longer.

He couldn't.

"Kate," he said again, but was unsure how to continue. She needed him and cared for him, she'd told him that much herself, but he knew better than to expect it to last.

Still, he had her in his arms, and at this moment he was too weak to deny himself. He'd dreamed of this too often. He'd take what Kate was offering. Kate raised her head to look at him questioningly. And hopefully.

In answer, he lowered his mouth and kissed her.

It was even better than he remembered. All those nights he'd tortured himself with memories of what it was like to taste her. He increased the pressure on her lips, molding them to fit his mouth perfectly. Perfect was all he could think as she opened her lips and he took advantage. She tasted of woman and goodness.

Feeling invincible, he scooped her up and stepped backward to his bed. He wanted her too much to worry about consequences. For once, he wouldn't calculate all the reasons he couldn't be involved with Kate.

To show her how much he needed her, Robert gave himself up to her. Kate struggled with his clothing, moaning her disappointment when her shaking fingers couldn't undo his shirt buttons. He stopped her with a finger against her lips and she lifted her eyes. Passion-filled eyes. "Slowly," he whispered and traced the outlines of her face. Her cheeks, her forehead. He kissed a tiny freckle she had at the corner of her mouth. There was no part of Kate that's wasn't beautiful. "There's no rush."

Kate smiled and stretched against him, offering her body. "As long as it takes," she teased, "to close the deal?"

"Exactly." He laughed and then he kissed her again.

He wanted to touch every part of her at once, but as he uncovered a shoulder or the top of a breast he got distracted and had to linger.

His Kate had beautiful breasts, he discovered as he pulled the green sweater over her head. Her black bra was all lace and sin. He cupped the fullness of one breast in his hand, watching as her nipple tightened, and then he stroked it. He liked the sound Kate made when he did that, so he repeated his actions slowly again and again. "I like the lace," he said, his voice thick. "Did you wear it for me?"

"Oh, yes," Kate said on a gasp as his mouth finally covered her nipple. "It's not exactly regular wear for nursing mothers." She smiled when she heard Robert chuckle. Who'd have ever imagined that Robert liked to laugh in bed? But then she forgot everything as his lips trailed down her stomach to her sensitive navel and his hands explored farther.

He was touching her everywhere and yet it wasn't enough. She couldn't possibly be close enough, have enough of him.

Robert smelled musky and masculine; she'd never been really aware how male a man could smell. His shoulders were so broad and strong that she couldn't resist sinking her teeth into them. She had the crazy, incredible need to devour him.

As Robert kissed her inside thigh, and Kate practically fainted with the heat of it, she realized that she was naked and writhing on the bed while he was still practically fully clothed. But then he trailed and teased.

his fingers along the inside of her thighs and she forgot how to think for a while. Finally, as his fingers began to explore her intimately and he began to kiss her breasts again, Kate took hold of his shoulders and pushed him away from her a little. "Stop," she said on a gasp as he continued to stroke her.

Robert raised a flushed face, his gaze falling briefly to her breasts, but then back to her face. "Stop what?" he asked as he inserted another finger inside her.

"Stop that." Kate wished her voice didn't sound so breathy and weak.

"Don't you like it?" Robert smiled a wicked lustful smile. "Or is this better?"

"Oh!" That was all Kate managed at first and she felt herself on the verge of explosion. She wanted him with her. "Stop," she ordered in a slightly more controlled voice. "I want you naked."

Robert's smile grew even more devilish. "Your every wish is my command."

Together they managed to remove his clothes and then Kate launched herself on top of him. She wanted to know what it was like to feel every inch of him against her bare skin. That wasn't enough, though, so she began to explore his body. But Robert didn't give her enough time. He rolled back on top of her and asked, "Now, where were we?" And he pressed his erection against her entrance.

"Oh, yes," she said on a sigh. "We were right there."

He entered her in a smooth stroke and then remained perfectly still. She understood completely. He possessed her; she possessed him. They kissed and smiled, but soon pounding pulses and heat and need were too much and they began to move. As Robert took over her senses, all she could think about was the joining of their two bodies, about how intimate the act of making love was. She wasn't sure if she'd ever made love so completely and uninhibitedly and she felt herself reaching the crest. Perfect was all she could think as she heard Robert cry out at the same moment she did.

HER HEAD RESTING on Robert's chest, Kate listened to the strong, even beats of his heart. With his arm around her, tucking her into him, she was happier than she'd ever felt in her life. She hadn't even known it was possible to feel this way.

She let herself imagine a lifetime of moments like this, of being with the man she loved more than anything. Raising her head, she looked at him, his strong jaw and sensual lips. She'd thought him uncaring and passionless once. It was hard to imagine. Robert opened his eyes and smiled at her.

She wanted to tell him she loved him but knew this was the wrong time. What they had was too fragile. She needed time with him to show him how much she loved him.

His house had proven that he was a man who didn't believe in love.

She was going to prove him wrong. "Wow," she murmured.

He ran a hand along her back and Kate arched against him like a cat. Or a well-satisfied woman.

He kissed her and she felt herself float.

"Maybe we'd better check on Sarah."

Kate sighed. Robert wasn't going to make this easy for her. "I'd rather stay in bed all day with you, but you're right." She sat up and stretched, noting with satisfaction how Robert's gaze followed her movements. "Why don't we take Sarah out for pizza?"

Robert got out of bed and found his jeans. Kate's mouth went dry as she watched him dress. "Sarah wants anchovies."

"Only on her half of the pizza then."

Kate glowed inside; for a moment she felt as if they were an old married couple. It was great. Dressing quickly, she went to the nursery and scooped a sleeping Sarah into her arms and kissed the top of her baby's head. She really could have it all if she trod carefully. If she didn't scare Robert off.

Sarah woke up and gurgled. With a happy baby in her arms and her body still humming from lovemaking, Kate wanted to spin around the room shouting, "Whee." But then she caught sight of Robert lounging at the door, observing mother and daughter. She buried her face against Sarah's to cover the emotions she knew were plain to see on her face. "Maybe you should pack a bag," Kate mumbled into Sarah's belly.

"What?" Robert asked.

"Maybe you should pack some things into a bag." She tried to shrug nonchalantly and managed some kind of odd quirk of her shoulders. "You could stay at my place. If you want to. All of Sarah's things are there—"

"Okay," Robert cut her off quickly. But he'd left the room by the time she'd gathered the nerve to raise her head and look at him.

"It's a start, Sarah, darling," she whispered to her daughter. "It's a start."

13

BY UNSPOKEN AGREEMENT, over the next two weeks Robert moved into Kate's apartment. He'd spent only one night at his place the first week and grumbled something about it being too quiet. As Kate made room for his clothes in her closet, she found herself humming.

She confided the news to Jennifer, who didn't look surprised and said, "It's about time." She shook her lovely head, her expression much softer than it had been in a long time. "I really hope it works out for you. You're giving me hope."

At the office she and Devlin had several disagreements about the budget of Boardroom Baby's second advertising wave. Once they were home, however, they left it all behind.

It was like a honeymoon, Kate decided. A little separate magical time she and Robert had all to themselves. Their secret little world that included Sarah.

When Sarah was three months old and Kate was back at Carlyle almost full-time, Kate was beginning to think it would turn out all right.

Except that Robert had never said he loved her. All of his actions said that he cared for her, but Kate wasn't sure if he cared for her the way she cared for him. His lovemaking was passionate and frequent—Kate's lack of sleep had little to do with the baby—but he might have been like that with all of his lovers.

Kate wondered about other women he'd had in his life. She suspected he must have been badly hurt in the past. She hoped that was the reason he was so slow to reveal his feelings for her.

She desperately wanted him as in love with her as she was with him.

But she was beginning to realize she didn't know how to go about making him fall in love with her.

"DAMN IT, man, woo her." Alan Blackwood stared at his friend in puzzlement and Robert shifted uncomfortably under his scrutiny. He hadn't really meant to ask Alan for advice about Kate, but he had. Alan and Betty had been together and happy for a long time.

Alan took another sip of beer and then began to explain, slowly, as if he were talking to a child. "Let me make sure I understand the situation. You're the father of the baby."

"Yes." Robert was glad to be back to the facts. Those he could deal with.

"And now you're living together?"

"Yes." This was getting easier.

"And the two of you are involved. You're having sex, you're not just roommates?"

"Yes."

Alan shook his head. "Damn, but you move quickly. The pair of you find out the truth and jump right into a relationship."

"Yes." Robert was glad Alan understood the situation so well and approved. Maybe he wasn't as bad at this as he thought.

Alan grinned and slapped him on the back. "Robert, my friend, you're screwing up. Women like to be romanced. Flowers, dinners, dates, shared confidences. I bet you haven't done any of that."

"No." He hadn't. It hadn't seemed necessary.

"You have to win her affections. Prove to her that she's important, not taken for granted. Trust me, Betty let's me know when I take her for granted. I bet you've never even asked Kate out on a date."

"No."

The two men sat back, considering. Alan finished his beer and checked his watch. "I have to go, so these are my final words—I've known you a long time and I've never seen you nuts over any woman before. This Kate Ross has to be something special. You deserve something special. Show her she's special."

ROBERT TURNED HIS KEY to unlock the door and entered the apartment. He was still surprised at how good it felt every evening to come home to Kate's condominium, to see her and Sarah. It felt like home.

It had been a month since he'd moved in. He'd picked up a bouquet of flowers for Kate as sort of an anniversary present. Maybe he should have done something more, he thought worriedly. He should have phoned Alan and asked him.

Coward, a little voice mocked him. He was afraid that this precarious situation wasn't going to last. Soon, unknowingly, he'd do something wrong and Kate would begin to fade from his life. He pushed away his ever-present worry. He'd deal with that when it happened. He was going to enjoy the present.

Maybe she'd never leave him, another little part of him whispered. Maybe if he just said, "I love you," and asked her to marry him, Kate would say yes. But he couldn't believe that. A lifetime had taught him not to believe that.

Putting the flowers on the antique dressing table Kate used as a hall table, he shrugged out of his coat and hung it in the closet. As usual, the living room was a shambles with magazines spread over the sofa and Kate's files covering the dining-room table. He put his briefcase on the table, as well. Trying to ignore the mess, he went to the nursery in search of her.

Kate was hovering over a complaining Sarah. "There you are," she practically snapped at him. She picked up their daughter and thrust her at him. "You try calming her—she's been fussing all day."

Instantly worried, he took his daughter and studied her little face. Sarah made a sound of recognition and waved an arm at him.

"Ssh, little girl," he crooned. His daughter settled contentedly in his arms, closed her eyes and fell asleep.

"Where were you five hours ago when she wouldn't stop screaming?" Kate demanded irritably.

"I was at the office," he answered reasonably, noticing how out-of-sorts Kate looked. Dressed in sweats, her hair was pulled back in a ponytail and she hadn't bothered with makeup.

"You're late," she continued. "You could have phoned."

"It's only seven," he said, wondering what was really going on here. "What is it, Kate?"

"Oh." She ran a hand through her hair, destroying the ponytail. To his horror, he saw that she was close to tears. "Sarah fussed all day and you were late and I didn't want to call you because switchboard would recognize my voice and wonder why I was always phoning you and Gina faxed over early numbers on Boardroom Baby and, while they're good, Grannie Goodspoon is keeping up—whoever helped them really hurt us—and I'd wanted tonight to be special and Mother invited us to dinner tomorrow night." The last was said on a wail and Robert felt fear clutch his stomach.

He knew all about the baby-food account and was doing his best to track down the culprit in Carlyle.

But Kate's family... What had she told them about him? Would they immediately see that he wasn't good enough for their daughter?

Still cradling Sarah, he took Kate's hand and led her to the living-room couch.

He sat next to her and continued to hold her hand. What Kate didn't know was that the gesture was as much for his comfort as hers.

"We'll go have dinner with your parents," he said with a lot more conviction than he felt.

Kate's words poured out. "Everything just sort of piled up on me today. When my parents invited me and Sarah to dinner and I didn't want to phone you at work, I realized that we've been sneaking around like we're cheating on our spouses. It's as if you're embarrassed to be involved with me. I haven't even told Anne about our living together."

"Kate, I'm not embarrassed." Robert was shocked. She couldn't really believe that, could she?

"Then what is it?"

How could he explain that it was for her sake that their relationship should remain a secret? When she got tired of this affair, there would be fewer explanations to make.

"It's as if you're planning for when we're no longer together." Kate spoke his reasons out loud. They sounded cold and terrible.

It wasn't what he wanted. He wanted Kate and Sarah. The more he thought about it, the less the revelation scared him. Suddenly he was filled with confidence and resolution. For some reason, Kate was imagining a future with him and for once he was going to take an emotional gamble.

"Kate, nothing would make me happier than for everyone to know that we're a couple."

"Really?"

"Yes. Now, why don't you go take a nice long bubble bath and I'll put Sarah to bed?"

Kate's smile was full of such curious hope that Devlin felt his heart fall even more firmly under her spell. "Look at what a mess I've made of the dining room," Kate said suddenly, as if to distract herself. "Let me just tidy up a little."

She grabbed her folders and tried to sweep them together. Gathering them into one big pile, she turned to place them on the buffet behind the table when she knocked over Robert's briefcase. "Damn. Nothing's going right today."

Robert stepped toward her. "Let me get that." But it was too late.

Kate was staring at the private investigator's report that had fallen from his attaché case. He could see as clearly as she could the name Kate Ross at the top of the folder.

Kate raised stricken eyes to him. "You had me investigated." Her voice was too soft, too quiet.

"I had everyone at Carlyle investigated," Robert corrected, hoping desperately that somehow he could make this right.

Kate was reading the pages. "But I was the main suspect. Because I was in charge of Boardroom Baby."

"That was the investigator's decision, not mine. Everyone with access to confidential information had to be looked at, including myself."

Kate flipped through the pages and sucked in her breath when she found a picture of herself and Sarah in the park. "How long has this been going on?" she demanded.

"A couple of months. We needed to give our mole every opportunity to believe we had lost interest so he could incriminate himself." Robert was scared. Kate was too still. He had wanted to tell her about the investigation, but Anderson had sworn him to secrecy. "Kate, it had nothing to do with us," he said fiercely when she still wouldn't look at him. He grabbed her by the shoulders, making her raise her face to him. "I knew you weren't guilty."

"What if I was, Robert? What if I had been selling Carlyle's secrets?" Her eyes glistened with unshed tears.

"But you wouldn't, Kate. It's not you. I know you." He had never for a moment suspected it was her. But he had the terrible feeling that he had missed something here, that Kate was slipping away from him even as he held her. "It was just business, Kate."

"Business." She broke free of his arms and strode away, as if she couldn't bear the touch of him. "How could you not tell me, Robert? How could you not have trusted me enough to tell me? What if I had been guilty? Would you just have turned over the file to Anderson, packed your bags and left me?"

"Kate, what you're saying doesn't make any sense. I knew you couldn't be guilty."

"That's not the issue." She turned on him, anger blazing across her face. "What if I was? Would you have helped me or walked away? I haven't pushed you about us because I thought there was some issue of trust that we hadn't resolved. That you were afraid to trust me. That someone had badly hurt you before and you didn't think I'd stick around through thick and thin. No matter what happened." She shook her head in disgust. "And now I learn that you don't trust me. You should have told me, Robert. You should have believed in me enough to tell me. I had hoped I was more to you than just some affair. I wanted so much more..."

Kate's last word broke on a cry and she collapsed onto the sofa, huddled into herself.

Robert felt his happy little world crumbling around him.

"I wanted you to pick me over Carlyle," she said in a muffled voice.

"I do, Kate. Oh, God, I do. You have to let me prove it to you." Robert thought his heart might burst out of his chest if she didn't look at him and tell him yes.

Instead, she shook her head and blew her nose. "Put the baby to bed," she said. "I need some time alone."

Alone. The word chilled him as never before. He had made a mistake. But how could he make Kate understand?

He left her as she'd asked him to and went into the nursery. His little girl's room. He loved being in here. He loved being with Kate.

He wanted to stay with Kate. He needed to stay with Kate.

Sarah complained as he put her in the crib. Letting her curl her tiny fingers around his index finger, he sat in the rocker next to her bed. Sarah wanted and needed him. He'd have to find a way to convince Kate of the same. The home they were creating together was filled with love—even though neither had acknowledged it.

Sarah fell asleep, loosening her grip on him, but Robert continued to sit there, staring at his daughter and thinking.

Finally, he felt Kate's presence at the door. Looking up, he saw her, beautiful and tired. Her confused emotions were spelled out clearly on her face. A few months ago he hadn't been able to read her, but now he could. He could barely remember the Kate Ross that had frustrated him so, the woman he had believed too impulsive, too ready to break all the rules. This woman had changed his life. Given him hope and a belief in the future.

"Kate." He stood to tell her how he felt. But the words didn't come. It was still too soon; he didn't want to scare her off.

Instead, he walked to her and held her. There was one way they communicated very well. He had always done better with actions than declarations.

She trembled in his arms and sighed. "Oh, Robert, I overreacted."

"Ssh." He patted her hair, wanting to take care of her. Never to make her worried or angry. "I'm sorry. I should have told you. It's just that this—you and me— is all new for me. I don't want to screw it up."

"Robert, we can make this—us—work. I know we can."

Kate looked at him, her face filled with emotion. Her eyes were shining and Robert was afraid she might cry.

He did the only thing he could think of. He kissed her.

It was like coming home. Kissing Kate was like a taste of heaven. No matter how often he touched her, tasted her, it always surprised him how right, how good it felt. He wondered how he could have lived before he'd made love to Kate. And each time he feared it might be the last time.

Never! She was his woman, the one he would grow old with—and he was going to prove it to her.

He broke off the kiss and scooped her into his arms. "Robert!" she exclaimed in surprise, but he cut off any further conversation with his lips, demanding entrance into her sweet mouth with his tongue. Kate wrapped her arms around his neck and responded passionately, wildly.

It didn't take any time for him to carry her to their bedroom. Breaking their kiss, he put Kate on her feet next to the bed, staring deeply into her eyes. They were dark, almost drugged looking as she stood on shaky feet, looking back at him with desire and curiosity.

The need to prove that he was the only man for her, the need to conquer had taken over. He could feel the heat between them and he suddenly wanted Kate naked. Grabbing hold of her sweat top, he raised it quickly over her head and then freed her breasts from her bra. Kate's lips parted with excitement as he gathered her exquisite, lush breasts into his hands, using his thumbs to caress her nipples. They pebbled pink and hard with his touch and he groaned. He loved how responsive she was to his attentions.

The blood was pounding in his ears, his body was demanding possession of Kate immediately. Control was completely gone.

He pushed Kate back on the bed, landing on top of her, barely registering her exclamation of surprise. Finally, he could put his mouth on her breasts, lips and teeth, tasting, swirling his tongue around the sensitive areolas, using his teeth to graze the undersides of her breasts.

Somewhere in the background he heard Kate moan. He felt her twist under him, but he wasn't willing to give up any control and he imprisoned her with his legs. That also allowed him to press his rampant erection against her. As he continued to torture her breasts with his mouth, he rocked himself against her.

"Robert!" Kate said on a gasp. "Let me—oh!" Her words died as he bit her very gently.

Then he raised his conquerer's face to her and kissed her hard on the mouth. He demanded everything from her, every secret, every wish. "This time is for me and you," he whispered. "Let me take control."

He didn't wait for permission. Tired of having Kate only half-naked, he pulled off her sweatpants and panties in one quick move. Her white socks stayed on and he thought she looked very sexy like that.

He explored his way back down her neck, pausing briefly to worship her breasts again and then moved to her lovely stomach. It was still ever so slightly curved after her pregnancy and he found it very erotic. When he tongued her naval, Kate jumped. He used his hands to arouse her further, around the side of her hips, down along her buttocks and her long legs.

When he began to trace the inside of her thighs toward the center of her need, and his, he raised his head to look at her. Her breath was coming in quick pants and he laved one nipple and then blew on it. "You're my woman," he said possessively. His fingers continued to tease her, circling the V between her legs.

Kate opened passion-filled eyes. "Yes."

"Always."

"Yes."

He entered her with two fingers. Kate climaxed and he covered her mouth with his own, swallowing her passion into him. He continued to stroke her, coaxing her along the waves for as long as possible. After she'd finished, he kept kissing her gently.

Finally, Kate broke away. "That was...do-the-right-thing Devlin at its best." She laughed softly. "You're still clothed. Not fair." She raised her arms as if to help him disrobe, but Robert stood. He could do it much faster himself.

Naked, he lay on top of her and entered her. Kate smiled at him and they began to move together.

"You're mine," he said and took them both over the top.

HER PARENTS waving goodbye, Kate strapped Sarah into the baby seat of the van and breathed a sigh of relief. Robert was holding open the door for her and impulsively she reached up and kissed him on the cheek. "Mmm, you smell like cigars."

"Your father invited me to have one on the terrace after dinner."

"And a talk?" she quizzed as she seated herself. She thought Robert had been fantastic throughout his ordeal with her parents. She'd found it more nerve-racking than the first time she'd had a boyfriend over to dinner, but Robert had handled the event with ease and charm. Of course, she really hadn't expected any less from him.

She'd crossed her fingers and prayed that he would like her family.

Her parents clearly approved of him. As they left the house, her parents had been grinning as if they'd won the lottery.

Well, some days she felt that way, too. She hadn't forgiven him for not telling her about the private investigator, but she was trying to understand him a little better every day. Last night, after their fight, she'd been afraid he'd leave her. Instead, he'd made love to her with a ferocity that had thrilled her. As if he'd been afraid it was for the last time and he wanted to remember everything about her. And for her to remember him. She remembered everything.

She needed to give him time. Time to become comfortable with the idea of them together forever. Time for him to fall in love with her.

How ironic that she—who loved challenges, the bigger the better, and always won—couldn't make it happen when it mattered most.

Robert looked very handsome in his dark suit and white shirt. Her father's eyebrows had shot up when he'd realized she'd brought home a man wearing a tie. Conservative, traditional Robert was her father's dream man. It's a good thing he didn't know Robert was the one responsible for getting her in the family way. She smiled to herself.

Robert turned his attention to her and as their eyes held, she felt the connection between them clear down to her toes. Robert smiled back at her, the line of strain easing on his face.

"Did Father grill you?"

"Yes. He wanted to know what my intentions were toward you."

"What? He didn't!" Kate felt herself blanch. What had possessed her father? He'd never even asked Todd such a question.

Robert gripped the steering wheel tightly. "Bill—" when had he begun calling her father Bill? Todd had never gone beyond Mr. Ross "—wanted to make his position clear."

"Oh, Robert, I'm so sorry." Kate buried her face in her hands.

Robert reached over and pulled her hands away, then squeezed her left hand gently. "He loves you, Kate—you and Sarah. He just pointed out to me how much better things would be if things were...official between us."

"You didn't tell him that you're Sarah's father, did you?"

"No, I thought we could leave that shocker for later. Bill thinks I became involved with you just before Sarah was born, but he also thinks I shouldn't be wasting your time if I'm not serious about you and the baby."

"It's my life," Kate spluttered.

"Now, Kate, he's only worried. Your single motherhood jolted your parents. And then you and me—well, your father thinks you don't have time to waste." His lips twitched. "I think your father thinks as you're a single mother you're not as marketable as you used to be."

Kate couldn't say anything but she did squeak.

"He's right," Robert said calmly.

"What do you mean?" Kate asked, holding herself very still. She was scared of what Robert might say next.

"It will be harder for you to find a husband as a single mother." Robert took a deep breath.

"I am not husband hunting."

"That's why we should get married."

The words were what she'd been longing to hear, but not how she'd wanted to hear them. She turned on him. "Because I won't be able to find another husband?"

"Yes. No. Your father made me think about the future. I'm not being fair to you or Sarah if I'm not willing to commit. And I want to be part of Sarah's life officially. So we should get married."

"Oh." Kate told herself not to be so disappointed. Todd had proposed to her over a romantic candlelight dinner and look where that had gotten her. Robert would keep his promises, that she knew beyond a doubt.

"Is this about last night? Is a marriage proposal your way of saying, 'I'm sorry I didn't trust you'?" Kate queried.

His eyebrows flared. "This is only about you and me and Sarah."

Because she wanted so much more from him, she probed. "You want to marry me because of Sarah?"

"Yes," he said, sounding pleased that she understood him. "You know how important family is to me."

"Yes."

Kate thought over his words. Robert shot her a look when she didn't say anything else. Good, let him sweat a little.

"Yes as in you'll marry me, or yes as in you know how I feel about families?" he finally asked.

She couldn't read his carefully neutral tone. "Yes, I know how important families are to you." Kate considered her options. This wasn't the kind of proposal she'd wanted from Robert, yet she should have expected it. This was her chance, it might not be romantic and pretty but she would have the time she needed to show Robert how she felt about him.

"Yes," she said. "I'll marry you."

Robert nodded the same nod whenever he'd concluded a successful business deal.

She really was going to have to teach him about the importance of showing some emotions: like pulling the car over to the side of the road and kissing her senseless. Still, all at once, Kate was happy. She had her chance.

14

"THAT'S SOME ROCK." Jennifer whistled. "You must have quite a nest egg tucked away."

"Is it too much?" Robert looked at the diamond and sapphire engagement ring with concern. He thought it was a style Kate would wear, but if Jennifer considered it too ostentatious... "She likes sapphires," he defended himself. He couldn't believe how nervous he was; it wasn't like him at all. Usually, he simply made a decision and took action. He was able to calculate possible responses and plan alternatives. But this time, the situation involved him and his feelings and he had never felt so out of control.

"Oh, no, Robert, it's beautiful. You know Kate's taste well. It's just...big." Jennifer patted his hand. Then she smiled at him. "Kate is going to love it."

"Are you sure? She didn't wear one...before."

"With Todd, you mean? I think that was part of the problem. They were far too reasonable and practical about their engagement. Now, this ring..." She tried it on and held it against the light. "This ring makes a statement. It says, she's taken. Hands off. Don't even think about it. Plus, what is it? Two carats?" she assessed professionally. "You're telling the world you're more than capable of looking after her financially. Very he-man. Macho."

Macho? Possessive? Robert could hardly believe Jennifer's words. In surprise, he realized she was right. With the engagement ring, he was staking his claim on Kate.

She was his woman.

God, that sounded good to him.

Jennifer was saying something. "Robert, I was only teasing." Impulsively, she hugged him. When she let go of him, he saw her wipe a tear away. "I'm so happy for the pair of you—and it's about time, too! You'll be good for her, Robert."

"I'm going to do everything I can for her and Sarah," he vowed. "They're more important to me than anything in the world."

"Of course they are. I've known that for a long time." She chuckled suddenly. "It's a good thing, too. Now Kate won't have to pay fees to the infertility clinic a second time."

"What?"

"Oh, don't you want more children?" Jennifer was flustered by Robert's silence. "I thought you and Kate would want to have another baby."

"I hadn't really thought that far ahead. Does Kate want more children?"

"Yes. That was always part of her plan. She prefers Sarah not to be an only child."

Robert felt poleaxed. Is that why she was marrying him—as a convenient sperm donor? So her children could have the same genetic makeup?

What if she were? It was a practical, sensible solution to her dilemma.

But he'd wanted to believe her yes came from her feelings toward him. That what she felt was more than lust and a passing infatuation. That she wanted to grow old with him.

He was a coward. If he'd been honest with Kate about his feelings for her, she could have let him down gently.

But was she really only marrying him because he was the father of her child—and the potential father of more?

He had to admit that his proposal could have been more polished, but he'd been so taken by the idea after Mr. Ross had put it in his head, he hadn't had time to plan his approach. Especially after he had almost blown it with Kate. If she said yes, he'd vowed never to let her regret it.

But he realized his usual practical, sensible method wasn't going to be enough. He wanted to make Kate love him.

And if she didn't?

Robert suddenly realized he wasn't going to marry Kate either for convenience or for Sarah. Tonight he was going to buy her roses, take her out for a romantic dinner and tell her he loved her and then ask her to marry him. If she felt even the smallest bit toward him as he felt about her, then he would continue to wait until he'd convinced her he was the best man for her.

And if she didn't even begin to feel as he did?

Robert pocketed the engagement ring. He wasn't going to settle for less.

His telephone buzzed, the call display showed Gina's extension.

"Robert, can you meet me in Ted's office right away? We have a small problem." Gina's voice sounded strained and frightened.

"I''ll be there in two minutes."

TWO HOURS LATER, Robert cursed. He'd checked and rechecked the Boardroom Baby figures but there was no doubt about it—they'd miscalculated. After the successful launch, profit figures were barely showing a break-even.

It was the product cost. He'd been analyzing the spreadsheets for hours and he'd found the error: the transposition of two numbers. A small mistake but in the hurry to speed up production it had slipped through.

To make any kind of profit from Boardroom Baby would mean Carlyle Industries would have to increase the price of the baby food, not an action that would reaffirm their position as a company that was honest about its product.

Carlyle Industries was about to catch a lot of flak. He took off his glasses and rubbed at the pain building behind his eyes. He picked up the papers and began to work backward, trying to figure out how this calamity had happened. Could it possibly have been another form of corporate sabotage? If not, then who was to blame?

He found the answer. The sudden rush of adrenaline jolted him upright. Then he frowned. It couldn't be. He followed the trail looking for any other possibility.

But there wasn't one. The blame could be directly assigned to one person.

Kate.

Her initials were all over the approvals on the incriminating documents. Why did it have to be her?

There might be other hands involved, but the approval was Kate's responsibility.

If only they hadn't been so rushed, this would never have happened. Robert realized that argument would never hold sway with Larry Anderson. No, what he needed to do now was take care of the situation. If the executive board learned of Kate's mistake, she'd be severely punished. More than her dream of becoming vice president would be gone.

He couldn't let that happen.

He loved her. When it came to choosing between Kate and anything else, Kate won. Suddenly he realized that was what she'd been trying to find out, what she'd been asking him all along. He finally understood.

He shoved the incriminating documents into a folder and locked it in his drawer.

He had a lot of work ahead of him.

KATE RUSHED INTO Devlin's office, staring at the sales printout in her hands. She couldn't keep her excitement to herself. "The orders have increased by twenty percent. And you said I wasn't a numbers person! These numbers I could learn to love! Robert, we have to go out and celebrate." She looked up. His office was empty.

It was curious how disappointed she felt at not finding him. That's what love did. She'd said goodbye to him—passionately—this morning and she missed him already. She had it really bad for Robert Devlin; she couldn't remember being this infatuated, even as a teenager. At least then it had been acceptable to look moonstruck and scribble the boy's name all over your desk. Try pulling that one off in the boardroom.

She'd write him a note inviting him to dinner. Candles and flowers. She would tell him... Yes, she had to tell him she loved him. Before they set a date for the wedding. She didn't think she could go through with the marriage if Robert didn't know how she felt, and if he didn't give her any indication that he could someday feel the same way.

Robert's desk was covered with papers. She searched through them, looking for something to write on. Curious, she held the financial statements for Boardroom Baby. Now, why was he going through them?

She tried a drawer. The top one was locked but in the second she found his personal notepaper and scratched out a note to him.

"Kate, are you there?" Jennifer peered through the door, slightly out of breath. "I'm glad I found you. What's the emergency executive meeting about?"

Kate wondered if she dared to sign her note with a heart. Distractedly, she asked, "Emergency meeting? What are you talking about?"

"Robert E-mailed me. It's not scheduled until five forty-five. I thought that was odd as I know that you leave at four-thirty these days." Jennifer looked down at her hands and then back at Kate and then looked away again. Kate realized that Jennifer was nervous. Calm, cool, collected Jennifer? "I thought his calling the meeting was strange because you're not on the E-mail distribution list. It's about Boardroom Baby."

That was very odd. And so was Robert's messy desk, all the documents scattered about. She began to examine them. "They're all financial statements on Boardroom Baby—shipping, packaging, advertising." Where were the product costs?

"Why would Robert call a meeting without informing you?" Jennifer asked in a meek voice.

Kate thought about the locked desk drawer; she could feel her urge to find out begin to override her common sense. She could ignore the rules of social and moral etiquette and pick the lock. No! She wouldn't really, would she? She considered his letter opener.

After she told him she loved him, no more subterfuge.

She held the letter opener in her hand, reconsidering. Should she invade his privacy? Something was going on and she needed to know what. It affected her relationship with Robert, she was sure of it. She set to work on the drawer.

"Do you think...could Robert have found something...bad and have called the meeting...?" Jennifer stumbled over her words.

Kate wasn't paying much attention. She had the

drawer open, but then the tone of Jennifer's voice intruded. "Jennifer, I love Robert. I know him. He wouldn't hurt me. You have to learn to believe in that."

Slowly Jennifer nodded. "You're right. You must be right," she said as if to herself. Then added desperately, "You and Robert are my hope that love can work out."

"It will," she assured her friend and returned her attention to the drawer. It contained the product-cost spreadsheets. Why was Robert hiding these? And then she saw the highlighted numbers. "No." Her hands shook as she saw what Robert had discovered about their baby—their other baby. Boardroom Baby was in trouble, because of her. Her approvals were all over the documents.

"Robert called the meeting because of this." Kate handed Jennifer the file. "Because of my mistake." Kate dropped her face into her hands. How could she have made such an error? She'd been under a lot of pressure and she'd been thinking about her soon-to-be-born baby, but that was no excuse.

It was her fault.

She was costing Carlyle Industries a lot of money.

Ouch.

She took a deep breath and opened her eyes. She needed to face the consequences as an executive. Then she saw the photograph. Robert kept a photo of her and Sarah in his drawer.

A burst of happiness spread through her body. This photograph proved that Robert...*cared*. That gave her hope. She beamed at Jennifer, who frowned.

"Kate, this is awful. Boardroom Baby isn't making—"

"—any money." Kate was still riding high from her discovery.

"Damn him. How could he do this to you?" Jennifer demanded, throwing the incriminating papers on the desk and stalking around the room. "How could he betray you for a promotion?"

Kate understood Jennifer's suspicions, but she also knew they weren't true. Robert wasn't like that. "Jennifer, whatever you're thinking about Robert, you're wrong."

"Kate, don't be deluded by your feelings for him. He's called a meeting without informing you. He has material on you that will not only guarantee you won't be vice president of marketing but could very well get you fired. Or worse."

"Or worse?" Kate said out loud, marveling at Jennifer's histrionics. What could be worse?

"It could ruin you forever if news gets out. If the old-boys' network spreads the word that you're unreliable, no company in the Northeast will hire you." Jennifer's words didn't frighten Kate as they once would have. If what Jennifer predicted came to be, she'd deal with it. Figure out something else to do. As long as she had Robert on her side, she was invincible.

Without one doubt, she knew Robert was her ally, every atom of her being knew that Robert couldn't betray her. She needed to prove herself to him. From what she knew of his background, she understood that no one had ever loved Robert the way she did. No one had been willing to sacrifice anything for him. She was and she would show him.

She took the incriminating pages. "Come on," she said to Jennifer. "It's time for a little surprise in the boardroom."

ROBERT LOOKED at his watch—5:47. Another minute and he'd head for the boardroom. He'd never been late to a meeting before, but this time he was about to use every dramatic and manipulative step he'd ever seen performed in such rooms. This was one scenario that had to unfold exactly as he played it.

Time.

With brisk strides he was at the door. This was it, he had to win. He entered the room.

Faces turned to him as one unit. While all of them, Swinson, Lipp, Diamente, Benson, Silver and Givens, had on their professional, only slightly interested facades, their expressions were belied by the electric attention in the air. He had their attention, especially Larry Anderson's. Anderson undoubtedly believed this was Devlin's move for the vice presidency. Well, it was.

Jennifer raised an eyebrow as Robert took the head of the long table.

"I'm assuming this is important," Anderson began. "I should be tucking into dinner now." The executives laughed dutifully at his regular-guy routine.

"It is. We have a problem with Boardroom Baby."

"Ridiculous." Silver twitched. "The sales figures are excellent."

"If there's a...concern," Jennifer said carefully, "why isn't Kate here? The pair of you are in charge, as far as I understood."

Robert knew Jennifer would be his toughest test. While he'd been busy with the paperwork all afternoon, he'd had a few minutes to worry over Jennifer. She might notice Kate's absence on the distribution list and query her. In order for him to win, Kate had to remain unaware.

"Kate is fully aware of the state of affairs. Because of her domestic situation and as more of this problem is my responsibility, it was logical for me to be the one to explain."

"Proceed," Benson demanded.

"The news on Boardroom Baby looks good, but as we know—" staring at Benson "—looks can be deceiving. Sales, shipping, marketing, consumer response are excellent, but we made a small mistake in our production costs which, when multiped by our volumes, means we're just breaking even."

A terrible silence gathered over the room as everyone turned toward Larry Anderson. All joviality disappeared from his hard face. "Are you telling me that Carlyle Industries isn't making a profit?" Anderson asked.

"Exactly."

"Who made this mistake?"

"I did," Robert answered his furious CEO.

"Robert!" Jennifer exclaimed loudly.

"You?" Lipp asked.

"You don't make mistakes," Benson said incredulously.

The door opened and Kate entered, stopping the clamor. She walked slowly and confidently to the head of the table to join Robert, put her briefcase on the table and clicked it open, pulling out some manila folders. Then she smiled her breezy, win-them-over smile. Robert felt himself fall even further under her spell. He glared at Diamente who had smiled back at Kate too eagerly.

"I'm glad I was able to settle things at home and return before Robert got too far. While I have several suggestions on how we can best present our price increases—" Kate opened one of her folders and passed out the appropriate memo "—first I want to state that the error was entirely my responsibility. Robert had nothing to do with it."

"That's not true," he said, wondering when she had become such an idiot. Anderson and the others would accept a mistake from him. They'd be glad of the chance to see him as human and fallible, but they'd crucify Kate. There was enough latent sexism in this room that the opportunity to discredit her would be seized.

"Surely you're not about to suggest that Kate is lying," Jennifer said. He realized they were playing him like a team.

"I'm sure Kate feels responsible because Boardroom Baby was her product from the start, but I was the one who made the miscalculation on the figures." He played his card. "You all know that I'm the numbers man." He distributed the faked documents he'd spent the afternoon working on. His initials were on the bottom left-hand corner of each sheet.

Kate let everyone study the spreadsheets before them. Benson's nose twitched as he looked at the incriminating numbers and then studied Robert.

To Kate, however, the forged documents filled her with confidence. Mr. Do-the-right-thing Devlin was willing to sacrifice himself for her. That meant he had to care about her a lot. She could wait for him to love her, if she had to. But it was time Robert Devlin learned how she felt about him. A public declaration had to convince him. She hoped.

Lipp turned pale and cleared his throat. "I should have seen this error. I take full responsibility."

"Arthur," Kate began, "you're being too generous. The mistake was my fault."

Robert ignored her and gestured to the group with his glasses. "As you can all see from the documents, we made an error in the product costs and despite the success of Boardroom Baby we're only breaking even. If we maintain our market share for the next six months, a minor price increase would be feasible and we can slowly pull the product into a greater profit margin."

"How did this happen?" Anderson demanded.

Kate let Robert go first, as she knew he would. "There is no excuse for what happened. It was a mistake caused by our tight deadline, but I should have been more careful."

"I should fire you for this," Anderson fumed.

"I can have my resignation on your desk before I leave tonight," Robert said stiffly.

Kate wondered if Anderson would be angry and stupid enough to actually accept Robert's offer. She held her breath as Anderson shook his head. "No, that would be an even bigger mistake than this Boardroom Baby disaster. Anybody have a cigarette?" Diamente pulled out a crumpled pack and Anderson lit up. "What do we do now?"

Kate tapped her folders. "I have new marketing plans here, but basically Robert is right. We have to continue as we are and increase our price very slowly." She took a deep breath and addressed Anderson personally. "I'm glad you appreciate Robert enough to know that losing him would be an even greater loss than what's happened to Boardroom Baby. But there is something else you need to know—"

"Kate," Robert pleaded. "There's nothing more—"

"There's a lot more to say and I should have said it earlier." Filled with nervous energy, she rose and began to pace the boardroom. "Robert lied when he claimed that the mistake was his—it was mine." At the surprised exclamations, she pulled out the original, highlighted printouts from her briefcase and handed them to Anderson. "Robert was covering for me because he thought...because he believed it was the right thing to do. But he's lying. Robert never saw this spreadsheet. The mistake is completely my responsibility."

"Kate." Robert spoke in an even, measured tone, but Kate could see the steel in his eyes. "You're wrong."

"See, even now he wants to protect me. He thinks you'll be easier on him than me. He thinks he should protect me. Which is a really sweet romantic thing to do, but Carlyle Industries is too important to Robert for me to let this happen."

"Kate, stop this."

"See, Robert always does what's right, what's noble. Even if it means putting everyone else before himself. I can't think of a better way of choosing your next vice president."

The room was completely still as everyone stared first at her and then at Robert. Kate found she was almost afraid to look at Robert, but she did. She could see anger in his eyes, but also confusion. Then he sighed and shook his head, turning to Anderson. "For some unknown reason, Kate has decided to make herself the scapegoat in this affair—"

"Are you calling me a liar?" she asked.

"No, of course not. You're just overly emotional about this...situation. You can't just throw away everything you've worked toward, Kate. It isn't right."

"It isn't right for you to take the blame for something I did. It's like you, Robert, but I can't let you. How could we ever have a future together with this between us?" Robert's eyes widened slightly in surprise and Kate continued in a rush. "A future with you is much more important to me than some silly old job. I love you. I want to marry you."

"Kate, you don't know what you're saying."

"I'm fully aware of every word I'm saying. I love you. I've loved you for weeks." She turned to all the shocked faces, all except for Jennifer's which wore a wide grin. "Robert is the father of my child. I love him desperately and want to marry him."

Every eye turned to Robert as he strode toward Kate. Her heart was hammering so loudly she couldn't focus on anything except Robert's handsome face. "Kate, why are you doing this?" he asked.

"Because I love you. Because I can't let you lie for me and ruin your own career. Because no one knows you like I do. You're the best man I've ever met. And if you feel even the slightest way toward me the way I feel about you...we could be very happy together."

"I love you," Robert said, pulling her into his arms. He kissed her senseless, not that she'd had many senses left by that point anyway.

Kate kissed him back with all her heart, wanting nothing more than to be with this man forever.

"Ahem." At the sound of Anderson's voice they broke apart. Kate felt herself flushing but she didn't care. With Robert still holding her hand, they faced their audience together. Diamente and Lipp looked bemused while Benson smiled in smug satisfaction. Anderson stared at the pair and at their clasped hands pointedly. Robert only held her hand more tightly. "I don't think the boardroom is exactly the place for this kind of thing, but these circumstances are extraordinary, so I'll excuse it this time. I want the pair of you to fix this problem with Boardroom Baby and then I'll make my decision about the vice presidency."

"That's it?" Benson squeaked, betraying himself.

"No, not quite," Anderson said and smiled. "You're fired."

Benson turned pale and then red. "F-fired! I haven't done anything!"

"That's why you're fired. I don't care that you are a relative—I've had enough of you and your big mouth." Anderson stood and glared at the little man. "I didn't mind when you snuck out of the office to play golf, but when I talked to your golf instructor and learned that he also teaches the Goodspoon executives, I knew I'd found our leak."

"But I never told George anything!" Benson protested. "He just asked a lot of questions about a lot of things..." Benson's nose twitched as he began to put his own mistake together.

"You can't be trusted, Benson," Anderson continued. "You didn't even know you were the one breaking my confidence. It was your over-inflated ego making you check out all the details of the Boardroom Baby campaign. You were looking for mistakes, and through sheer arrogance and stupidity you revealed our plans to Grannie Goodspoon. If you leave now, you'll discover my secretary has a very attractive package for you to sign off on." Anderson smiled dryly. "It includes free golf lessons."

As a group they watched Benson slink out of the room.

"Now, back to what I was saying." Anderson fixed his attention on Kate and Robert.

"I must admit I haven't found Devlin's and Ross's behavior to be at all professional throughout this entire meeting—each lying to me to protect the other. I don't ever want to experience anything like this again! I also think there's something you've forgotten, Devlin."

"What?" Robert was damned if he was going to apologize to the old man. He had Kate and all he wanted to do was leave.

"Ms. Ross has announced that she loves you. I think you're supposed to propose now," Anderson said with a smile.

It felt right, Robert realized as he reached into his pocket and pulled out the ring box. Him and Kate. She looked at him hesitantly as he opened up the box and pulled out the ring.

"Kate, I love you. Will you marry me?"

"Oh, yes!" He slipped on the ring and then kissed the tips of each finger. "Oh, Devlin, I don't know what to say—"

He silenced her with his mouth and Kate gave herself up to him.

Anderson called out, "Best merger I've seen in years!"

_____Epilogue_____

THE VICE PRESIDENT of marketing, North America, considered the promotion budget. Henderson was being too conservative in her calculations. You had to spend some money to make money.

The sounds of a little girl laughing broke the silence. The clock on the immaculate desk read five forty-five as Sarah Devlin came racing into the office with all the enthusiasm and speed that she'd inherited from her mother. "You're working too late," she squealed as she hurled herself into the parental arms.

"You *are* working too hard," Kate gently chided from the door. "It's dinnertime." She smiled at Robert as she walked across the room and kissed him. When she would have broken contact, he held her to him and continued to explore her mouth. "I'm a hungry man," he whispered against her lips.

"Robert, there are children present," she complained softly and then smiled again as his hand stroked her pregnant stomach. He could hardly believe his good fortune—how his life had changed ever since he had gotten himself involved in Kate's messy, complicated, wonderful life. He'd never really been alive until he'd fallen in love with Kate. He still marveled over the day when she had publicly declared her love for him in the boardroom. Who else but Kate would have thought of such a gesture? Or known that her public declaration would finally make him believe that he could be loved.

Now they were having another baby. Despite the ultrasound, they hadn't wanted to know the sex of the child. Kate, however, was convinced it was a boy and she called him R.J., for Robert Junior. Whenever he heard Kate use the name, he felt incredibly powerful and proud. His family.

It was everything he'd ever dreamed of but never thought he could have.

Kate had shown him how.

She peered past his shoulders at the promotion figures and frowned. "Those are too low—"

Robert snapped the file shut. "No spying on the competition."

"I would never spy," Kate said indignantly and then laughed, "unless of course the file was open right in front of my nose, then I couldn't help but look."

Ever since Kate had quit Carlyle Industries to open up her own consulting firm, Robert had to be careful. On many occasions she worked for Carlyle's competition, although she had never accepted any of Grannie Goodspoon's offers. Still, he knew Kate and her roving eye.

After he had become vice president, Kate announced she was leaving Carlyle Industries. He'd been worried, but she'd assured him that she agreed he'd be the better vice president. She just didn't think she should work for him. She said she was more of an ideas person, anyway, and contract work would give her more time with the children. The plural of that word had stopped him.

He smiled at his family and realized that he, Robert Devlin, had it all.

EVER HAD ONE OF THOSE DAYS?

TO DO:

☑ late for a super-important meeting, you discover the cat has eaten your panty hose

☑ while you work through lunch, the rest of the gang goes out and finds a one-hour, once-in-a-lifetime 90% off sale at the most exclusive store in town (Oh, and they also get to meet Brad Pitt who's filming a movie across the street.)

☑ you discover that your intimate phone call with your boyfriend was on company-wide intercom

☑ finally at the end of a long and exasperating day, you escape from it all with an entertaining, humorous and always romantic Love & Laughter book!

ENJOY
LOVE & LAUGHTER™
EVERY DAY!

For a preview, turn the page....

Here's a sneak peek at
Colleen Collins's RIGHT CHEST, WRONG NAME
Available August 1997...

———————

"DARLING, YOU SOUND like a broken cappuccino machine," murmured Charlotte, her voice oozing disapproval.

Russell juggled the receiver while attempting to sit up in bed, but couldn't. If he *sounded* like a wreck over the phone, he could only imagine what he looked like.

"What mischief did you and your friends get into at your bachelor's party last night?" she continued.

She always had a way of saying "your friends" as though they were a pack of degenerate water buffalo. Professors deserved to be several notches higher up on the food chain, he thought. Which he would have said if his tongue wasn't swollen to twice its size.

"You didn't do anything...bad...did you, Russell?"

"Bad." His laugh came out like a bark.

"Bad as in *naughty*."

He heard her piqued tone but knew she'd never admit to such a base emotion as jealousy. Charlotte Maday, the woman he was to wed in a week, came from a family who bled blue. Exhibiting raw emotion was akin to burping in public.

After agreeing to be at her parents' pool party by noon, he untangled himself from the bed sheets and stumbled to the bathroom.

"Pool party," he reminded himself. He'd put on his best front and accommodate Char's request. Make the family rounds, exchange a few pleasantries, play the role she liked best: the erudite, cultured English literature professor. After fulfilling his duties, he'd slink into some lawn chair, preferably one in the shade, and nurse his hangover.

He tossed back a few aspirin and splashed cold water on his face. Grappling for a towel, he squinted into the mirror.

Then he jerked upright and stared at his reflection, blinking back drops of water. "Good Lord. They stuck me in a wind tunnel."

His hair, usually neatly parted and combed, sprang from his head as though he'd been struck by lightning. "Can too many Wild Turkeys do that?" he asked himself as he stared with horror at his reflection.

Something caught his eye in the mirror. Russell's gaze dropped.

"What in the—"

Over his pectoral muscle was a small patch of white. A bandage. Gingerly, he pulled it off.

Underneath, on his skin, was not a wound but a small, neat drawing.

"A red heart?" His voice cracked on the word *heart*. Something—a word?—was scrawled across it.

"Good Lord," he croaked. "I got a tattoo. A heart tattoo with the name Liz on it."

Not Charlotte. Liz!

Let's Celebrate!

LOVE & LAUGHTER™

invites you to
the party of the season!

Grab your popcorn and be prepared to laugh
as we celebrate with **LOVE & LAUGHTER**.

Harlequin's newest series is going Hollywood!

Let us make you laugh with three months of terrific
books, authors and romance, plus a chance to win a
FREE 15-copy video collection of the best romantic
comedies ever made.

For more details look in the back pages of any
Love & Laughter title, from July to September,
at your favorite retail outlet.

Don't forget the popcorn!

Available wherever
Harlequin books are sold.

 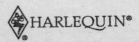 HARLEQUIN®

Look us up on-line at: http://www.romance.net

LLCELEB

Take 4 bestselling love stories FREE

Plus get a FREE surprise gift!

Special Limited-time Offer

Mail to Harlequin Reader Service®

> 3010 Walden Avenue
> P.O. Box 1867
> Buffalo, N.Y. 14240-1867

YES! Please send me 4 free Harlequin Temptation® novels and my free surprise gift. Then send me 4 brand-new novels every month, which I will receive before they appear in bookstores. Bill me at the low price of $2.90 each plus 25¢ delivery and applicable sales tax, if any.* That's the complete price and a savings of over 10% off the cover prices—quite a bargain! I understand that accepting the books and gift places me under no obligation ever to buy any books. I can always return a shipment and cancel at any time. Even if I never buy another book from Harlequin, the 4 free books and the surprise gift are mine to keep forever.

142 BPA A3UP

Name	(PLEASE PRINT)	
Address	Apt. No.	
City	State	Zip

This offer is limited to one order per household and not valid to present Harlequin Temptation® subscribers. *Terms and prices are subject to change without notice. Sales tax applicable in N.Y.

UTEMP-696 ©1990 Harlequin Enterprises Limited

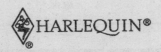

HARLEQUIN WOMEN
KNOW ROMANCE
WHEN THEY SEE IT.

And they'll see it on **ROMANCE CLASSICS**, the new 24-hour TV channel devoted to romantic movies and original programs like the special **Harlequin** Showcase of Authors & Stories.

The **Harlequin** Showcase of Authors & Stories introduces you to many of your favorite romance authors in a program developed exclusively for Harlequin readers.

Watch for the **Harlequin** Showcase of **Authors & Stories** series beginning in the summer of 1997.

If you're not receiving ROMANCE CLASSICS, call your local cable operator or satellite provider and ask for it today!

Escape to the network of your dreams.

ROMANCE CLASSICS

Free Gift Offer

With a Free Gift proof-of-purchase
from any Harlequin® book, you can receive
a beautiful cubic zirconia pendant.

This stunning marquise-shaped stone is a genuine cubic
zirconia—accented by an 18" gold tone necklace.
(Approximate retail value $19.95)

Send for yours today...
compliments of 🔶HARLEQUIN®

To receive your free gift, a cubic zirconia pendant, send us one original proof-of-
purchase, photocopies not accepted, from the back of any Harlequin Romance®,
Harlequin Presents®, Harlequin Temptation®, Harlequin Superromance®, Harlequin
Intrigue®, Harlequin American Romance®, or Harlequin Historicals® title available at
your favorite retail outlet, together with the Free Gift Certificate, plus a check or money
order for $1.65 U.S./$2.15 CAN. (do not send cash) to cover postage and handling,
payable to Harlequin Free Gift Offer. We will send you the specified gift. Allow 6 to 8
weeks for delivery. Offer good until December 31, 1997, or while quantities last. Offer
valid in the U.S. and Canada only.

Free Gift Certificate

Name: _____

Address: _____

City: _____ State/Province: _____ Zip/Postal Code: _____

Mail this certificate, one proof-of-purchase and a check or money order for postage
and handling to: HARLEQUIN FREE GIFT OFFER 1997. In the U.S.: 3010 Walden
Avenue, P.O. Box 9071, Buffalo NY 14269-9057. In Canada: P.O. Box 604, Fort Erie,
Ontario L2Z 5X3.

FREE GIFT OFFER   084-KEZ

ONE PROOF-OF-PURCHASE
To collect your fabulous FREE GIFT, a cubic zirconia pendant, you must include this
original proof-of-purchase for each gift with the properly completed Free Gift Certificate.

084-KEZR